Chloe

MORE GRAPHIC NOVELS AVAILABLE FROM charmz

AMY'S DIARY #1
"SPACE ALIEN... ALMOST?"

AMY'S DIARY #2
"THE WORLD'S UPSIDE DOWN"

AMY'S DIARY #3
"MOVING ON"

STITCHED #1
"THE FIRST DAY OF THE REST OF HER LIFE"

STITCHED #2
"LOVE IN THE TI
OF ASSUMPTIO

CHLOE #1
"THE NEW GIRL"

CHLOE #2 "THE QUEEN OF HIGH SCHOOL"

CHLOE #3
"FRENEMIES"

CHLOE #4
"RAINY DAY"

ANA AND THE
COSMIC RACE #
"THE RACE BEGI

SCARLET ROSE #1
"I KNEW I'D MEET YOU"

SCARLET ROSE #2
"I'LL GO WHERE YOU GO"

SCARLET ROSE #3
"I THINK I LOVE YOU"

SCARLET ROSE #4
"YOU WILL ALWAYS BE MINE"

G.F.F.s #1
"MY HEART LIE
IN THE 90s"

G.F.F.s #2
"WITCHES GET THINGS DONE"

MONICA ADVENTURES #1

MONICA ADVENTURES #2

MONICA ADVENTURES #3

SWEETIES #1
"CHERRY SKYE

SEE MORE AT PAPERCUTZ.COM

Chloe

Carnival Party

Story by Greg Tessier
Art by Amandine

NEW YORK

To community groups and volunteers, just as impassioned as inspirational creative forces, whom it'll always be worthwhile to help and support to your utmost.
Because communicating fully with a foreign exchange student creates a real window to the world...
Long live the exchange of cultures and ideas, as well as all those who seek them!
–Greg

A big thanks to Pierre and Kaouet, the fabulous wrap-up team!
And then, for this volume that's all about community work, it's impossible not to thank Drac, Sam, David, and Nekomix, of course!
Thank you to a super team: Jésus and Mrs. Perspective for their sage advice; Pierre for his unforgettable job in the "Frying pan" and for sharing the long hours wrapping this up; and, of course, Gregory for his ever-lovely adventure with our little Misty!
To Fleurette, this tenth volume for your ten years
–Amandine

Chloe

CHLOE #5
"Carnival Party"

GREG TESSIER—Story
AMANDINE—Art and Color (vol.9), Text, Art and Colors (vol.10)
JOE JOHNSON, NANETTE McGUINNESS—Translation
BRYAN SENKA—Lettering
MARK McNABB—Production
JEFF WHITMAN—Editor
JIM SALICRUP
Editor-in-Chief

Special thanks to FLORA BOFFY

Charmz is an imprint of Papercutz.

PB ISBN: 978-1-5458-0143-7
HC ISBN: 978-1-5458-0142-0

Printed in China
June 2020

Charmz books may be purchased for business or promotional use.
For information on bulk purchases please contact Macmillan
Corporate and Premium Sales Department at (800) 221-7945 x5442

Distributed by Macmillan
First Charmz Printing

Second week of winter break...

Blin Family
DING

HEY, GOOD MORNING, FATOUMA! CHLOE WILL BE HAPPY TO SEE YOU. SHE GOT HOME FROM HER GRANDMOTHER'S BARELY AN HOUR AGO.
COME AND WARM UP.
THANK YOU, MRS. BLIN.

FATOU!

I WAS ABOUT TO CALL MARK AND YOU SO WE COULD MEET UP SUPER EARLY TOMORROW. I'VE MISSED YOU BOTH SO MUCH!

NOT TO MENTION, I REALLY NEED YOUR HELP WITH THE REPORT ON GETTING INVOLVED... I HAVE NO IDEA. IT'S A HORRIBLE TOPIC!
THAT'S EXACTLY WHY I CAME BY TONIGHT. YOU DIDN'T ANSWER MY TEXTS.

OH, YEAH, I HAD NO RECEPTION AT MY GRANDMOTHER'S AND AFTERWARDS, I TOTALLY FORGOT TO CHARGE MY CELLPHONE.
IN ANY CASE, I HAVE A THOUSAND THINGS TO TELL YOU AND--

CHLOE, I'M SORRY BUT I WON'T BE ABLE TO JOIN YOU. I'M GOING TO MY AUNT'S FOR THE WHOLE WEEK. I FOUND OUT YESTERDAY... I WON'T BE BACK TILL SUNDAY.

HEY, HEY, HEY! HELLO, EVERYBODY!
UH...

ARE MY DARLING CHILDREN IN THE HOUSE?
DADDY!

AHHH, THERE'S ONE OF THEM! AND WHERE'S YOUR SISTER, SON?
I'M WITH FATOUMA, WE'RE TALKING.

GOOD EVENING!
HI, KIDS!
I HAVE GREAT NEWS TO TELL YOU.

CHLOE, ARTHUR... YOUR FATHER MANAGED TO GET A FEW DAYS OFF JUST FOR YOU!
SO WE WON'T BE APART FOR SEVEN LONG, BEAUTIFUL DAYS...

AND I'M WARNING YOU, WITH THE SCHEDULE I'VE CONCOCTED FOR US, THE THREE OF US ARE GOING TO HAVE AN AWESOME TIME!
GULP!

WHAT DID I DO TO DESERVE THIS?!

Endurance

From the get-go, there's no downtime...

-MMMM?-

OUT OF BED, SLEEPYHEAD! IT'S TIME.
COCKA-DOODLE-DOO!

HUH?! THIS IS WRONG. IT'S WAY TOO EARLY!

?
UP, UP, UP!
NO ARGUING... THE EARLY BIRD GETS THE WORM.

UH... WHAT KIND OF BREAKFAST IS THIS?

VITAMINS TO GET A GOOD START FOR THE DAY.

WE NEED STRENGTH FOR OUR MORNING JOG!

UH... IT'S JUST... UNFORTUNATELY... UNFORTUNATELY, MY EXERCISE CLOTHES ARE DIRTY...

-TSSK!- YOU HAVE EVERYTHING YOU NEED HERE, MY LITTLE MISTY!

HUFF!
PUFF!
HUFF!

ISN'T THIS **GREAT?!** WE'RE BREATHING FRESH AIR, RIGHT?
MMM YEAH... IT'S SO COLD WE'RE THE ONLY ONES OUTSIDE THIS EARLY.
LOOK, DADDY. I'M GOING SO FAST! **WAH-HOO!**

SMELL THESE TREES FULL OF LIFE...

THAT POND OVER THERE...

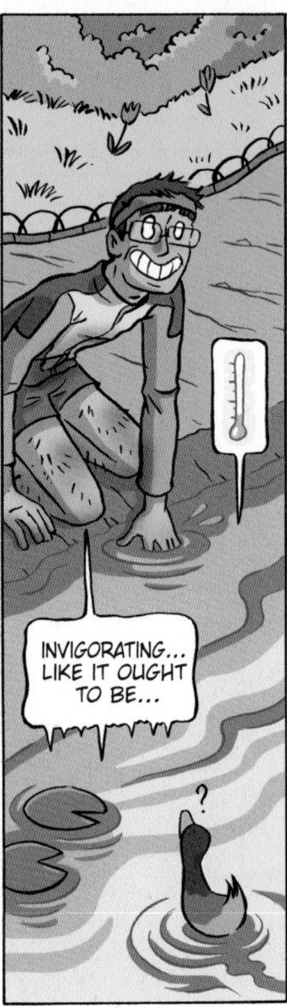
INVIGORATING... LIKE IT OUGHT TO BE...
?

??
IT'S SUCH A JOY TO COMMUNE WITH THE NATURE SURROUNDING US!

WHEW! HOME AT LAST!
WAP

LOOKS LIKE SOMEONE'S FEELING SORE.
YES, IT'S NO BIGGIE. A NICE SHOWER AND I'LL BE FINE...

DON'T WORRY. I'LL MAKE YOU BOTH A NICE, FORTIFYING MEAL BEFORE WE GET THE AFTERNOON PROGRAM UNDERWAY.

WHAT A PAIN! I'LL NEVER LAST A WEEK LIKE THIS.

IF ONLY IF I DIDN'T HAVE THIS AWFUL REPORT, TOO... I DON'T EVEN KNOW WHEN I'LL FINISH IT!

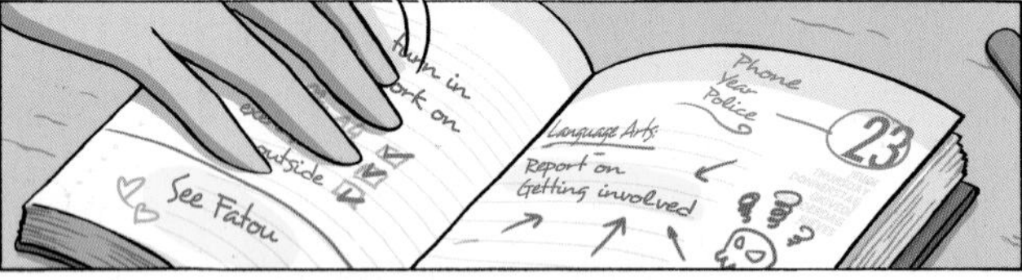

See Fatou
Phone
Year
Police
23
Language Arts
Report on Getting involved

WE SHOULD'VE WORKED TOGETHER, FATOU! WHY DID YOU ABANDON ME LIKE AN OLD SOCK?
PFFF. "INVOLVEMENT," THAT'S INSPIRING ABSOLUTELY NOTHING IN ME.

TIME TO EAT, CHLOE. MOM'S HOME!
HERE WE GO AGAIN...

fish sticks

LOOK WHAT I MADE FOR THE KIDS, FLO!

GOOD JOB, HONEY... I THINK I'LL HAVE TO LET YOU ENJOY THIS PLEASANT MOMENT YOURSELF, UNFORTUNATELY. I'LL WOLF DOWN A SALAD ON MY WAY BACK TO THE OFFICE.

UHHHH...

YOU OKAY, MISTY?

WHY WOULDN'T SHE BE?! SHE'S EATING AN AWESOME MEAL HER AWESOME DAD FIXED OUR FIRST AWESOME DAY TOGETHER!

YES, THAT'S RIGHT... I'M JUST HAVING SOME ACHES AND PAINS, THAT'S ALL. WE'RE HAVING A GREAT TIME WITH DAD.
YEAH, IT'S SUPER AWESOME!
OKAY, PERFECT!

?

That afternoon, the activities continue non-stop...
I'D TOLD YOU THIS VACATION WOULD BE UNFORGETTABLE!
AVIARY
EXIT
MONKIES

IT'S GOOD BEING WITH YOU, KIDS. IT'S REJUVENATING FOR ME!

OINK! OINK!

IT'LL BE DARK SOON... IT'S TIME TO GO HOME MAYBE, ISN'T IT?

THIS TIME THE DAY IS REALLY OVER!

SO, AFTER SPORTS, SOME COMFORT... WE STILL HAVE TIME TO PLAY A BOARD-GAME BEFORE YOUR MOTHER GETS HOME.
HUH?! UH... I HAVE TO WORK ON MY REPORT AND...

COME ON, CHLOE, SAY YES!

FINE, OKAY...

YEAH! AWESOME!
GOOD JOB, SON!

I WON AGAIN! YIPPEE!
YEAH, THAT'S BEGINNER'S LUCK...

YES!
THAT'S UNBELIEVABLE!
FAR

Our young heroine can't take it much longer, so she has to find help...
IT'S TIME TO GO WALKING WITH DADDY, CHLOE!
BAM BAM BAM

THANKS, UNCLE STEVE. ON MY WAY...

UH, NO! I ABSOLUTELY MUST GO SEE UNCLE STEVE FOR MY GUITAR LESSON! MY TEACHER'S ON VACATION, AND HE'S SUBBING FOR HIM.

IT'S IMPORTANT THAT I DON'T LOSE GROUND! YOU'LL TELL DAD, RIGHT, ARTHUR?

SORRY, DADDY DEAR, BUT I NEED TO BREATHE A LITTLE...

YIKES, ALL I NEEDED WAS THOSE THREE SNOT-NOSES!

IT REALLY ISN'T VACATION ANYMORE IF I RUN INTO THE WORST GIRLS FROM SCHOOL.
AM I DREAMING OR DID WE JUST SEE CHLOE?
PFFF! SHE RAN OFF TO HIDE AGAIN LIKE SOME BIG, FAT COWARD...
WE HAVE MORE IMPORTANT STUFF TO DO THAN SEARCH FOR THAT NERD!

COME ON, GIRLS, WE'VE GOT TO GET READY FOR SCHOOL. THE TRENDIEST STORES AWAIT US!
...

YOU SEE, IT'S REALLY COMPLICATED...

I USED GUITAR LESSONS AS AN EXCUSE BECAUSE I JUST COULDN'T LEAVE. I CAN'T TAKE IT ANYMORE, IT'S HORRIBLE!

BUT I LOVE DAD! I DON'T UNDERSTAND WHAT'S GOTTEN INTO HIM.
HE WANTS US TOGETHER ALL THE TIME, FOR US TO DO THINGS TOGETHER, TO HAVE FUN TOGETHER... BUT YOU CAN'T FORCE THOSE KINDS OF THINGS.

I HAVE THE FEELING YOUR FATHER'S HAVING SOME SORT OF MIDLIFE CRISIS!
HE WANTS YOU TO KEEP ON BEING A LITTLE GIRL BY HIS SIDE.

I DON'T EVEN HAVE TIME TO DO MY HOMEWORK, IT SUCKS...
TWANG

DON'T YOU WORRYYYY, MY LITTLE CHLOEEEE! A LOVING FATHERRRR WON'T STAY A BOTHERRRR...
JUST TELL HIM HOW YOU FEEEEL, AND IT'LL BE A DONE DEEEEAL!
YOU'RE PROBABLY RIGHT! I'LL TRY TO FOLLOW YOUR ADVICE.
IT'LL DO WONDERS FOR REEEEAL!

ALL RIGHT, BE BRAVE! I'LL MANAGE TO EXPRESS MYSELF.

AHHH, THERE SHE IS!
QUICK! GO FIND YOUR BATHING SUIT, CHLOE. WE'RE HEADING TO THE POOL!

DAD, I JUST WANTED TO TELL YOU--
GET IN, SON!

SINCE I'M A LITTLE OLDER, I'D MAYBE LIKE TO... WELL...

OF COURSE YOU CAN GO ON THE WATERSLIDE. I KNOW YOU'RE TOO OLD FOR THE WADING POOL!

THAT'S NOT IT...
I'D LIKE--

THAT'S FINE! NO WORRIES, YOU CAN DO THE DIVING BOARD, TOO!

SIGH. I'LL GO GET MY STUFF.

COME PLAY, CHLOE. IT'S SO AWESOME!

SPLASH
HAHAHA

SO, YOUNG LADY, AFRAID OF THE WATER?

DAAAD...
ADMIRE THE BACKSTROKE ANTHONY BLIN-STYLE! THERE'S NOTHING BETTER!

LOOKS LIKE SOMEBODY WANTS TO RACE ME?!
FFLISSS

GO!
FLOC
FLOC
FLOC

GO, DADDY! FASTER!
ERF!
URF!
IRF!
?
?
?

OH, HEY, CHRIS?! WHAT A SURPRISE TO RUN INTO YOU HERE!
OH, ANTHONY!

IT'S BEEN AGES SINCE WE SAW YOU AT JUDO.
I'D RATHER COME RELAX HERE. I PILE UP MY LAPS. THAT CALMS ME THE BEST!

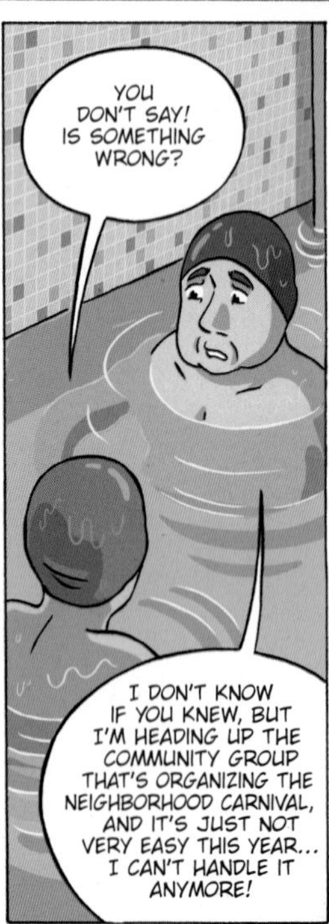
YOU DON'T SAY! IS SOMETHING WRONG?
I DON'T KNOW IF YOU KNEW, BUT I'M HEADING UP THE COMMUNITY GROUP THAT'S ORGANIZING THE NEIGHBORHOOD CARNIVAL, AND IT'S JUST NOT VERY EASY THIS YEAR... I CAN'T HANDLE IT ANYMORE!

IF THAT'S ALL IT IS... LISTEN, TOMORROW I'LL COME WITH THE KIDS AND HELP OUT!
THEY'LL LOVE IT, WON'T YOU, ARTHUR?
YES!
TAP TAP
GLUG!

UH... WHAT'S A CARNIVAL?

YOU SEE, ARTHUR, A CARNIVAL IS A BIG FESTIVAL WHERE PEOPLE PARADE IN COSTUMES...

WELL, IT'S MOSTLY AN EVENT WHERE EVERYONE LOOKS RIDICULOUS IN POORLY MADE COSTUMES.

HA HA! DON'T LISTEN TO YOUR SISTER! IT'S A NICE MOMENT OF SHARING, THAT'S ALL!
BY THE WAY, DON'T YOU HAVE A REPORT TO PREPARE ON GETTING INVOLVED, CHLOE? THIS COULD BE A GOOD OPPOR-TUNITY TO--
RUB RUB

I DON'T SEE THE CONNECTION!

HAVE YOU EVER BEEN IN THE CARNIVAL, DADDY?
NOT YET, WE HAVEN'T BEEN LIVING HERE VERY LONG, YOU KNOW.

WE CAN MAKE UP FOR THAT, THEN, BY GETTING INVOLVED ALONG WITH CHRIS AND HIS FAMILY.
I CAN ALREADY PICTURE US IN COSTUMES!

ARTHUR POTTER, ARTHUR BOND, SUPER ARTHUR... IT'LL BE UNFORGETTABLE!

SURELY...

Chloe doesn't know what to think!

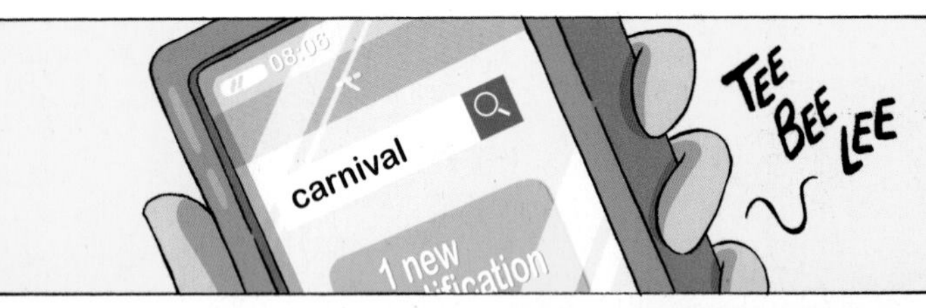
carnival
1 new
TEE BEE LEE

Anissa Bodier had added three new outfits on her page The Queen of Fashionistas.

WANT TO PLAY A GAME, CHLOE?
UH, NO, THIS TIME I'M GOING TO BED.

HUH, BUT IT'S ONLY 8 O'CLOCK?!
UHH... YAWN! WOW, I'M YAWNING ALREADY.
SORRY, I'VE GOT TO REST TO BE GOOD TO GO TOMORROW.

I UNDER-STAND! WE HAVE A BIG DAY AHEAD... THE CARNIVAL NEEDS US!

NOK
NOK

YOU SEEM OUT OF SORTS, MISTY. AM I WRONG?

CLAP
NO, NO, I...

CHLOE! NONE OF THAT WITH ME... YOU'RE NOT ENJOYING YOUR VACATION WITH YOUR FATHER?
WELL... SO... WELL... I DON'T DARE TELL HIM, BUT HE'S PROPOSING LOTS OF THINGS I DON'T NECESSARILY LIKE.

YOU KNOW, YOUR DAD MISSED YOU A LOT WHILE YOU WERE GONE. HE MADE IT A TOP PRIORITY NOT TO LET YOU OUT OF HIS SIGHT FOR THE REST OF HIS VACATION.
WITH THAT STUPID CARNIVAL ON THE AGENDA... AS IF I'M 5 YEARS OLD!

DID YOU TELL HIM HOW YOU FEEL?

I TRIED TO, BUT I'M AFRAID I'LL HURT HIS FEELINGS. IT'S MAKING DAD SO HAPPY TO SPEND TIME WITH US... I DON'T WANT TO DISAPPOINT HIM.

IT'S IMPORTANT TO EXPRESS WHAT YOU FEEL TO GUIDE THE OTHER PERSON SO YOU'LL SHARE SOME MOMENTS YOU BOTH LIKE.

BUT THEN, MAYBE BY EXPERIENCING THEM IN YOUR OWN WAY, THE ACTIVITIES PROPOSED BY YOUR FATHER MIGHT SEEM MORE INTERESTING TO YOU, NO? YOU HAVE TO BE ABLE TO DEAL WITH THINGS AS THEY ARISE. SOMETIMES THEY HOLD LOVELY SURPRISES FOR US...

DAD REALLY IS KIND OF THE CHAMPION OF SURPRISES... *HEE-HEE!*

MY NOTEBOOK
OF CAREERS
OF TORTURES
SPORT
Frozen ears and nose
Rain + glacial wind
MUD
More MUD
Even more MUD
Running in the middle of winter
= the idea of the century (by dad).
VISITS
0655285
ZOO
0655285
Entry into a
LOOONG, boring walk...
GAM
What an AWFUL time!
GROAN
Arthur VS Dad
RECREATION
MUNICIPAL POOL INFO
The pool will be open during the school break.
Hours: 10:00am – 6:00pm
Two hours of misery, water, and embarrassment!
TO DO
REPORT
With dad always under foot
+ ZERO motivation
+ That blasted carnival
+ Abandoned by Fatouma
⟹ 100% FAILURE
Yes!
-10%
0%
100%

Discovery

The Blin family is going to encounter a whole new universe...

SCRCH SCRCH
I DIDN'T KNOW THIS PART OF THE NEIGHBORHOOD AT ALL. LUCKILY, CHRIS EXPLAINED TO ME HOW TO FIND THEIR OFFICE!

SCRCH SCRCH
THE ENTRANCE SHOULD BE HERE... OR MAYBE IT'S DOWN THERE INSTEAD, AT THE END OF THE CUL-DE-SAC?

UNLESS IT'S THIS DOOR?! BUT THERE'S NO BUZZER...

?
?
SQUEAK!
BOOM
BIM
BAM

OH, IT'S YOU!
COME ON IN, IT'S OPEN.

WELCOME.
THANKS. WE WERE ANXIOUS TO SEE HOW YOUR ORGANIZATION WORKS.

WHOA, IT'S SO SCARY!
TELL ME ABOUT IT...

IT LOOKS REALLY... UH... FULL.
YOU'RE GOING TO MEET OUR AWESOME TEAM OF VOLUNTEERS.
WE'VE GOT VISITORS, MY FRIENDS!

...
GUYS!
WHY ARE YOU SHOUTING?
CALM DOWN, CHRIS!

WE HAVE REINFORCEMENTS FOR THE HOMESTRETCH FOR CARNIVAL PREP. LET ME INTRODUCE ARTHUR, CHLOE, AND THEIR DAD, ANTHONY.

HE'S ANN MARIE?!
NO, HE LOVES MONEY.
?

THAT'S GOOD, ME, TOO!
HEY, WHAT'S FOR LUNCH?

OKAY, OKAY, LET'S GET BACK TO WORK.
I THINK HE WANTS HIS FORK...

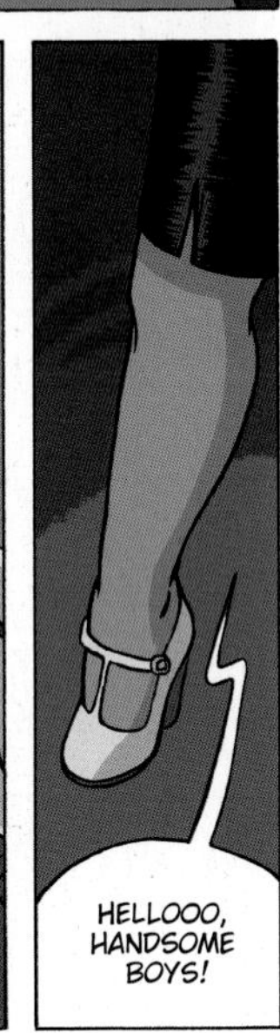
HELLOOO, HANDSOME BOYS!

AHHH, THERE'S OUR BEAUTY!
SUCH CHARM!
YOU GOTTA ADMIT, SHE'S A HECKUVA GAL!

UH, JACKIE, THIS IS--
FLAP
FLAP
THERE'S NO NEED, CHRIS, I HEARD EVERYTHING!

DELIGHTED, YOUNG MAN.

HELLOOOOOOO, ARTHUR!
SMOOCH!

HOW ARE YOU, CHLOE? THESE SCOUNDRELS HAVE WELCOMED YOU POLITELY, AT LEAST?
AND ME?
YES, THANK YOU, MA'AM!

JACKIE'S THE ONLY WOMAN IN OUR COMMUNITY GROUP AND THE YOUNGEST OF OUR ACTIVE MEMBERS. SHE'S THE ONE WHO SEES TO THE MONEY AS TREASURER.

SPEAKING OF WHICH, I HOPE THESE NEWCOMERS WON'T COST US TOO MUCH?
BILL

SO, YOU TALKING BUDGET IS PERFECT TIMING. I HAVE TO GO FIND A FEW EXTRA COSTUMES FOR THE PARADE, IN FACT. SO, I'LL NEED THE ORGANIZATION'S CHECKBOOK TO...

ABSOLUTELY NOT! NO NEED FOR EXTRAVAGANCE! AUNT JACKIE HAS A BETTER IDEA!

PARTY TIME
COSTUME RENTALS/STREAMERS/PARTY SUPPLIES

YOU SEE, KIDS, WE CAN STEAL IDEAS RIGHT AND LEFT AND RECREATE THEM AT THE WORKSHOP.
GOT IT!
IT'S AWE-SOME!

GOOD JOB, CHLOE! YOU HAVE TALENT!

WE DON'T HAVE LOTS OF MONEY, BUT DON'T WORRY, WE'LL GRAB A LITTLE BITE ON THE WAY BACK.
A SPECIAL GIFT FROM THE ORGANIZATION!

THIS TOP WILL BREAK HEARTS AT SCHOOL.

IT'S A KNOCK-OUT!
OH, SHOOT! ANISSA AND LESLIE, NOT THEM...

SPEAKING OF WHICH, I WONDER WHERE NAOMI IS? USUALLY, THEY'RE INSEPARABLE!

YEEAAH! WE'LL DRESS UP TOGETHER!

Despite that sighting, our young heroine immediately gets back to work...
DEAR FRIENDS, IT'S TIME TO BRING NEW LIFE TO OUR OLD STOCKPILE.

WHETHER WE WEAR THEM OR LEND THEM OUT, WE NEED MORE UP-TO-DATE COSTUMES TO DUST OFF THIS CARNIVAL.
+ old drapes

HERE, MISTER!
THANKS, LITTLE BOY!

YOU SEEM LOST IN THOUGHT, MY LITTLE MISTY?
MMMM...

"MY LITTLE MISTY"?

THAT'S MY NICKNAME..

1...

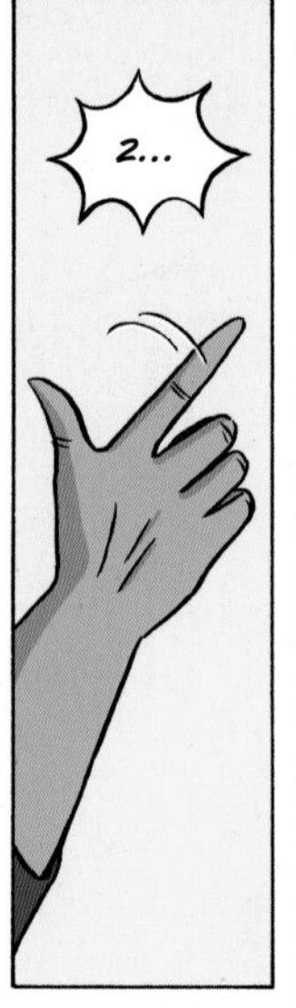
2...

UH 1, 2, 3...

PEOPLE SAY THAT I LOOK PRETTY, BUT I WOULDN'T BE A MISTY, IF I DIDN'T LOOK LIKE THAT...
LA LA LA...
JEEZ, I'M GONE FIVE MINUTES AND THINGS GET OUT OF HAND!
COME ON, ELLIOTT, I GOT NO TIME TO WASTE, MOVE IT! YOU'VE HAVEN'T COME IN A LONG TIME, BUT YOU KNOW PRETTY MUCH EVERYBODY...
DON'T LET YOURSELF BE INTIMIDATED BY JACKIE. YOU KNOW HOW SHE IS!
YEAH, IT'S FINE...
YOU SON'S LOOKING MORE AND MORE LIKE YOU, CHRIS.
HE'S SO TALL! HOW OLD IS HE?
TWELVE.
THOSE LITTLE CRITTERS SURE GROW UP FAST!
BY THE WAY, ANTHONY AND I THOUGHT HE AND CHLOE WOULD MAKE A GREAT TEAM!
HUH?!

YOU COULD'VE MAYBE ASKED MY OPINION?

I--

I THOUGHT I WAS JUST GOING TO HELP YOU, YOU!
AND WITH A GIRL, TOO... GREAT, WE CAN TALK NAIL POLISH AND FASHION SHOWS, LIKE WITH LOUANNE'S BABYSITTER.

CAREFUL, YOUNG MAN!
WATCH THAT TEMPER.

I'LL BE DELIGHTED TO SHOW YOU OTHERWISE, ELLIOTT!
WE'RE GOING TO WORK REAL WELL TOGETHER, I'M SURE OF IT.

YOU KNOW, I DID SOME SKETCHES OF COSTUMES WITH JACKIE, AND THEN, WE PINNED THEM ALL UP FOR INSPIRATION AT THE OFFICE...
AND WE REDID THE OUTFITS!
YES, YES, THAT'S WHAT WE DID.

WELL, THIS CARNIVAL FOR FIVE-YEAR-OLDS DOESN'T SOUND SO BORING!

HMMM... I DON'T KNOW WHAT YOU'RE TALKING ABOUT! *HEE-HEE!*
UH, NO, IT'S A CARNIVAL FOR ADULTS...

TEE BEELEE
Messages
Fatouma: I hope your report's coming together. Good luck!

YOU'RE RIGHT, FATOUMA. I'VE GOT TO GET GOING!

YOU'LL SEE, I'LL DO MY BEST.

Their work quickly bears fruit...
I'VE BROUGHT YOU TOGETHER TODAY BECAUSE ELLIOTT AND I'D LIKE TO GET TO KNOW YOU BETTER AND FIND OUT WHERE PROBLEMS MIGHT EXIST, IF THERE ARE ANY, OF COURSE.
SO MY ASSOCIATE AND I HAVE PREPARED INDIVIDUAL QUESTIONNAIRES TO FILL OUT. THEY'LL BE ANONYMOUS, DON'T WORRY.

THIS KIND OF QUESTIONNAIRE, AS THEY EXPLAINED TO US IN CIVICS CLASS, LETS US MAKE A TRUE APPRAISAL AND BRING OUT THE CRITICAL ELEMENTS.

...

SNNORRRRE

AH, THAT'S A GOOD IDEA FOR SURE! I CAN'T WAIT TO FILL OUT CHLOE AND ELLIOTT'S FORM.
EXACTLY, JACKIE!
I'LL TAKE ONE RIGHT NOW.
OH, YES, ME, TOO!

GOOD JOB, SON. GOOD INITIATIVE!

THANKS!

THERE, THAT'S THE LAST ONE.
HEY, CHLOE! WHY DID YOU SAY WE PREPARED THE QUESTIONNAIRE TOGETHER? YOU DID IT ALL ON YOUR OWN.

I DID IT BECAUSE I'M CONVINCED YOU'LL GIVE ME A HAND GOING OVER THEM...

YOU SEEM MIGHTY SURE OF YOURSELF!

NOTHING'S EVER SURE, BUT I SAW YOU WERE REALLY TOUCHED WHEN YOUR DAD CONGRATULATED YOU EARLIER.

IT'D BE GREAT IF WE COULD KEEP WORKING ON THIS PROJECT TOGETHER, DON'T YOU THINK?
HMMM...

DO YOU AGREE TO HELP ME?

MISTER CHRIS! MISTER CHRIS!

TAC
TAC
OH, NO! NOT HER!
HUH?
NAOMI?! WHAT'S GOING ON?
WHAT'S GOING ON? WHAT'S GOING ON IS I CAN'T TAKE YOUR DAUGHTER ANYMORE!
WHAT HAVE YOU DONE NOW, *LOUANNE*?
IT'S NOT ME, DADDY, IT'S HER!

BABYSITTING A KID AS FULL OF HERSELF AS SHE IS... THANKS, BUT NO THANKS! YOU CAN HAVE HER BACK. I'VE GOT BETTER THINGS TO DO ON MY VACATION!
YOU'RE A WITCH!

THESE KIDS HAVE SPUNK! SHE REMINDS ME OF MY *JOSIE*...

YOU KNOW MY LITTLE SISTER'S BABYSITTER?
SHE'S ONE OF THE WORST MEAN GIRLS AT MY SCHOOL!

IF SHE SEES ME HERE WITH YOU ALL, I'M DOOMED.

WHY, I RECOGNIZE THAT VOICE!

I DON'T BELIEVE IT!? WHAT A JOY TO SEE YOU, CHLOE... MY DAY WASN'T A TOTAL WASTE AFTER ALL.
SO, PREPPING FOR THE CARNIVAL AND ALL? A DORK WITH A BAND OF DORKS, THAT MAKES A LOT OF SENSE!

ENOUGH WITH ALL THIS RACKET! WHAT ARE YOU DOING HERE? ANNOYING, CHLOE?
OF COURSE I'M ANNOYING HER.

AND SOON THERE'LL BE THREE OF US DOING SO. SHE KNOWS THAT...
SEE YOU SOON, KID!

KISSES IN ADVANCE FROM ANISSA AND LESLIE! *HA, HA, HA!*

WHO IS THAT AWFUL PERSON? A FRIEND OF YOURS?
IT'S NOTHING, JACKIE. LET'S GO REJOIN THE OTHERS!

I'M SORRY, DADDY...

DON'T GET UPSET WITH HER, PLEASE, IT'S NOT HER FAULT. NAOMI IS JUST CRAZY.
SHE REALLY IS CRAZY!

I JUST TOLD HER THAT HER CHEAP MAKEUP WOULD RUIN HER SKIN. IT'S FULL OF WEIRD ADDITIVES, AND SHE GLOBS ON LOADS OF IT...

AND IT'S UGLY, TOO!

WOW, YOU SEEM VERY INFORMED FOR YOUR AGE!
SHE'S MOSTLY A PAIN IN THE BUTT...

HEE-HEE!
BLLB

YIKES, IT'S THE HOMESTRETCH BEFORE THE CARNIVAL, AND NOW I DON'T HAVE ANYONE TO BABYSIT LOUANNE!

THIS LITTLE LADY WILL STAY WITH US. THAT'LL GIVE US A LITTLE MORE FEMININE PRESENCE, WE NEED IT...

SHE WON'T BOTHER YOU?
I THINK SHE'S PRETTY MUCH FOUND HER ROLE ALREADY.

NO MORE TIME TO WASTE, THEN!
SO, I'LL GO OVER THE QUESTIONNAIRES TONIGHT.

FINE... OKAY... WE'LL GO OVER THE QUESTIONNAIRES TONIGHT!

YES!

WE'RE ON AN ADVENTURE, BOYS!
EEEEEK!

MY NOTEBOOK OF CAREERS
AT LAST!
ENCOUNTERS
awesome
DISCOVERIES
The Carnival Association
$
The president (it doesn't seem easy all the time...)
The treasurer (she IS a little stingy!)
TEAMWORK
Please insert your completed questionnaires in the ballot box provided.
Signed: Chloe and Elliott.
I hope we'll get actual answers...
CREATING
My prickly work tool.
TO DO
REPORT
Oof! I still haven't made much progress, but now I have tons of ideas!!!
0%
100%
(so long as Anissa and company leave me alone...)

Taking Action

As D-Day approaches, the moment has come to take a few steps...
HUSH! LET'S LISTEN TO CHLOE AND ELLIOTT...
DO YOU HAVE ANY IDEA WHAT THEY'LL PROPOSE TO US?
EH? YOU THINK THEY'LL **OPPOSE US**?!
Carnival Meeting
BE BRAVE! YOU CAN START.
OKAY... AFTER MULTIPLE READINGS OF THE QUESTIONNAIRES, WE PULLED OUT TWO BIG THINGS TO THINK ABOUT..
FIRST, THERE'S A GROWING LACK OF FUNDS.
NOT FOR LACK OF OVERSIGHT, THOUGH...
SECOND, THERE ARE FEWER AND FEWER VOLUNTEERS, SO WE LACK MANPOWER.
UH, YEAH, WE CAN'T BE EVERYWHERE EITHER...
BASED ON THESE RESULTS, WE'VE DECIDED, THEREFORE, TO CREATE TWO TEAMS.
THE FIRST ONE WILL CANVASS BUSINESSES AND NEIGHBORHOOD ASSOCIATIONS TO FIND OUT IF THEY'D LIKE TO BE PARTNERS AND HELP US A LITTLE FINANCIALLY.
THE OTHER TEAM WILL BE RESPONSIBLE FOR ACTIVELY RECRUITING NEW VOLUNTEERS ESPECIALLY FOR THE EVENT!
WHAT'S MORE, WE HAVE A LITTLE PLAN FOR MOBILIZING IN LARGE NUMBERS...

SO YOU'D BE UP FOR HELPING OUR ASSOCIATION BY LOANING OUT A FEW OF YOUR COSTUMES?
IT'D BE HARD TO PARTICIPATE IN IT OTHERWISE...

WE'RE OKAY FOR THE THREAD AND FABRICS, BUT THEY'LL BE FREE, WON'T THEY, MISS?
Stitched Shop
YES, YES, NO WORRIES! I UNDERSTAND THAT'S IMPORTANT TO YOU.

DO YOU THINK YOU COULD TALK WITH ALL THE PARENTS YOU'LL SEE BEFORE SUNDAY?
OF COURSE, YOU SWEET LITTLE THING! YOU'RE SO CUTE...
SHE OBVIOUSLY DOESN'T KNOW YOU! *HA HA!*
Recreation Center please

Beauty Shop
UH... THIS ISN'T FOR ME, YOU KNOW... BUT COULD YOU LET US USE A BIT OF YOUR MAKEUP FOR THE SUNDAY CARNIVAL?
SURE, IT WOULD BE GOOD ADVERTISING FOR US!

I FINALLY GET TO MEET YOU! YOU'RE THE CHLOE I SPOKE TO ON THE PHONE, RIGHT?
YES, THAT'S ME, **MRS. ADRIANA**!

JUST KNOW, IT'S VERY MUCH MY PLEASURE TO PARTICIPATE IN YOUR EVENT. MY RESIDENTS WERE ONBOARD FROM THE GET-GO!

I HAVE AN IDEA, LET'S GO SEE THEM IN THE GAME ROOM. I THINK THEY'VE CREATED A LITTLE SHOW FOR US.
HEH HEH, I'M IN ON THE SECRET!

TOOTOOOOO TOOTOO- TOOTOOTOO-TOOTOOOO
TOOTOOTOOTOOO - TOOTOOTOOTOOTOOTOO
TOOT

IT'S TIME I SERIOUSLY THINK ABOUT A RETIREMENT HOME...

WHY ARE THE GRANNIES DANCING LIKE THAT, DADDY?
HEE-HEE!

OH! I EAT, SLEEP, AND BREATHE BRAZILIAN MUSIC!

OKAY, WE DESERVE A LITTLE BREAK, TOO!

While preparations are fully underway, a certain few, however, seemed very determined not to let themselves be overlooked...
THE FIRST ONE TO FINISH HIS SET OF POSTERS OWES THE OTHER ONE A PRIZE!
HEY, YOU'RE CHEATING! YOU ALREADY STARTED!

SO IT REALLY IS TRUE, NAOMI WAS RIGHT!
SO, EYESORE, YOU'RE GETTING READY FOR CARNIVAL FROM WHAT I SEE?

CARNIVAL
SUNDAY
YOU LIKE DRESSING UP TO LOOK RIDICULOUS, CHLOE?
YOU KNOW THAT'S ALREADY THE CASE EVERY DAY!

HAHAHA
HAHA

IT'S WEIRD, I'D HAVE SWORN FESTIVITIES HAD BEEN CANCELED THIS YEAR...
SCRIITCH

WHATEVER! JOKE AS MUCH AS YOU LIKE, EVERYTHING'S PRACTICALLY WRAPPED UP FOR SUNDAY!

AND WHY ARE YOU STALKING CHLOE, HUH?

OH, A VALIANT KNIGHT, IT'S SO TOUCHING!
PFFF!...
TOO BAD IT'S ALREADY TOO LATE.

TAKE A LOOK BEHIND YOU!

SO IT'S HERE?

YES, MOM! YOU'LL SEE. THAT PLACE IS SO, SO SEEDY IT STILL GIVES ME GOOSEBUMPS...
YOU CAN START THE INSPECTION, MR. BOURDEAU.

GUESS!
WHO'S HE? WHAT'S HE DOING AT OUR OFFICE?

I'M THE CODE ENFORCEMENT INSPECTOR, YOUNG MAN.
MY COLLEAGUE HERE WAS ALERTED BY HER DAUGHTER THERE WERE A FEW IRREGULARITIES IN THIS AREA. SO, I'VE COME TO SEE WHAT'S GOING ON!

BUT NOTHING'S GOING ON HERE!
IT'S A LONGSTANDING COMMUNITY GROUP...
LET'S LET THE EXPERTS WORK. BYE-BYE!
FROM WHAT I SEE OF THIS BUILDING'S EXTERNAL CONDITION OF DETERIORATION, I CAN'T EVEN IMAGINE WHAT THE INSIDE MUST BE LIKE.
CLIC
THAT'S LIKELY THE PROBLEM.

IF IT CONTINUES LIKE THIS, I THINK I WON'T HAVE ENOUGH FORMS FOR MY REPORT... WHAT A RAMSHACKLE CONDITION! YOU WERE RIGHT TO INFORM ME.

AH, I HEAR STEPS! IT MUST BE THE CHILDREN BRINGING MORE VOLUNTEERS.

OKAY, A LITTLE BREAK WON'T HURT YOU, COME HAVE REFRESHMENTS WITH US.

NO, THANK YOU!

WHAT DO YOU MEAN NO?!

DON'T BE FINICKY WITH ME...
I'VE BROUGHT YOU SOME NEW FOLKS, MY FRIENDS!
CHEERS!

OKAY... THAT'S ENOUGH NOW! I'M MR. BOURDEAU, FROM CODE ENFORCEMENT, AND I'VE COME TO INSPECT THE PREMISES AND VERIFY THE SECURITY PORTION OF YOUR MARCH.
AND WHAT I'VE SEEN SO FAR IS ENOUGH TO TELL ME THAT YOU CAN STOP WITH THIS FARCE ALREADY.

YOUR CARNIVAL WILL BE CANCELED ONCE AND FOR ALL!

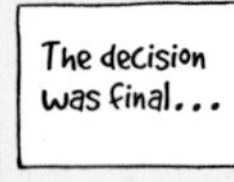
The decision was final...

YES, CHRIS. GOT IT. I UNDER-STAND.

CLIK
WELL?

SO, WELL... IT'S JUST AS WE FEARED. UNFORTUNATELY, THE CARNIVAL WON'T HAPPEN THIS YEAR.
WE CAN'T DRESS UP?

THIS IS MY FAULT... THIS HAPPENED BECAUSE OF ME...
COME BACK, CHLOE!

IF I DIDN'T KNOW NAOMI, THIS NEVER WOULD HAVE GOTTEN TO THE INSPECTOR...

COME ON, IT'S CLEARLY NOT YOUR FAULT. THAT MAN SIMPLY ENFORCED THE RULES. THAT HAS NOTHING TO DO WITH YOU, MY LITTLE MISTY.

I UNDERSTAND IT'S HARD TO ACCEPT, BUT GETTING INVOLVED IN A CAUSE ALSO RUNS THE RISK OF IT SOMETIMES NOT SUCCEEDING.

THE ONLY ONES TO NEVER FAIL ARE THOSE WHO DON'T TRY DOING ANYTHING. FAILURE IS JUST AS EDUCATIONAL AS WINNING, YOU KNOW.

BEING DISAPPOINTED IS NORMAL, BUT THAT DOESN'T ERASE THE GOOD TIMES SPENT WITH ELLIOTT AND THE OTHERS, AM I RIGHT?
MMMM....

A few details still have to be settled before ending this lovely adventure...

THANKS FOR COMING! WE'VE BEEN ASKED TO CLEAR THE PREMISES BEFORE THE DAY'S END.
SINCE WE HAVE NO OFFICE, A DUMPSTER WILL COME BY THIS EVENING TO TAKE THE STUFF TO THE DUMP...

HI, ELLIOTT.
WHAT A PAIN.

THIS WASN'T ALL FOR NOTHING. LOTS OF PEOPLE ARE COUNTING ON US.
I DON'T KNOW ABOUT YOU, BUT I REALLY DON'T WANT THINGS TO END LIKE THIS.

UNFORTUNATELY, WE DON'T HAVE ANY SOLUTION, HON.

LOUANNE
MAYBE WE COULD THINK ABOUT IT?

WHATEVER. IT'S OVER AND THAT'S IT!

NO WAY, LOUANNE IS RIGHT! THAT'S WHAT I WAS GETTING AT.
WHAT IF WE EACH TOOK THE TIME TO SAY WHAT WE MOST WANT, A LITTLE LIKE WITH THE QUESTIONNAIRES?

THERE! GETTING INVOLVED MEANS FAILING SOMETIMES, BUT IT'S ESPECIALLY ABOUT NEVER GIVING UP.

I- I'D LIKE US TO BE UNITED AGAIN...
I'D LIKE THE CARNIVAL TO BE A HUGE PARTY!
I WANT TO WEAR MY COSTUME ON SUNDAY!
I'D LIKE TO KEEP WORKING WITH YOU ALL.
ME TOO, AND WITH OUR NEW RECRUITS.
I'D LIKE EVERYONE WHO COUNTED ON US TO KNOW THEY MADE THE RIGHT CHOICE.

Each person does their part after that...
CHRIS, WHAT PRECISELY DOES THE INSPECTOR'S E-MAIL SAY?
TAP TAP

HE SAYS WE MUST VACATE OUR OFFICE RIGHT AWAY BECAUSE IT'S TOO RUN DOWN.
AND HE ADDS THAT WE COULDN'T, IN ANY CASE, HOLD THE CARNIVAL BECAUSE WE DIDN'T HIRE ENOUGH SECURITY GUARDS TO CONTROL THE PARADE ROUTE.

HMM... I'M GOING TO DO SOME NETWORKING. I SHOULD BE ABLE TO GET MY CLIENTS TO PUT A TRUCK AND A WAREHOUSE AT OUR DISPOSAL.
WE COULD STORE ALL OF OUR MATERIAL AND COSTUMES THERE.
HERE, DADDY, THAT'S SO YOU CAN TAKE IT WITH YOU!

I HAVE A GREAT-NEPHEW WHO WORKS IN A SECURITY COMPANY. MAYBE HE COULD HELP US...
LET'S WORK THESE DIFFERENT CHANNELS AND QUICK! WE DON'T HAVE MUCH TIME LEFT.

PFFF!... WE'LL BE HURRYING EVERYWHERE AGAIN!
LOOK AT THAT! BOYS DON'T LIKE ACTION ANYMORE NOW?
LOUANNE
HEE-HEE!

Every minute counts now...
PACK IT TIGHT, FELLOWS! EVERYTHING'S GOT TO GO IN.
Hector Transport

LISTEN, LISTEN! I'M BACK FROM MY NEPHEW'S... AND... AND... AND THEY'RE OKAY WITH PROVIDING SECURITY FREE OF CHARGE!

DOES THAT MEAN THE CARNIVAL ISN'T CANCELED ANYMORE?
WAIT, CHLOE!

THERE STILL WON'T BE ENOUGH OF THEM TO COVER THE WHOLE PARADE ROUTE...

DARN IT! WHAT'LL WE DO THEN?

NOTHING'S KEEPING US FROM SHORTENING THE ROUTE! NOBODY WHATSOEVER WILL KEEP US FROM THROWING THIS PARTY. OUR PARTNERS BELIEVE IN US!

BRA... BRAVO, MR. PRESIDENT!
WHAT DID HE SAY?

HONK HONK
OKAY, LET'S GET BACK TO WORK! THE BOXES WON'T WAIT.

VVVVRRRRR

THAT'S A FUNNY FLOAT FOR OUR PARADE!
I FOLLOWED YOUR EXAMPLES BY CALLING ON MY ENTOURAGE...

JACKIE, LET ME INTRODUCE MARK, MY BEST FRIEND. HE'S GOING TO UPDATE YOUR OLD COMPUTER. HE'S THE KING OF COMPUTER SCIENCE!
AS FOR *PEARL*, SHE RUNS A MAKEOVER SHOP, SO SHE CAN HELP US MAKE THE BEST COSTUMES IN THE WORLD
AND UNCLE STEVE, HIM, OH, HE'S JUST UNCLE STEVE!

I'M ANTHONY'S BROTHER. WE'LL PROMOTE YOUR EVENT, BELIEVE YOU ME! I HAVE SOME MUSICIAN BUDDIES WITH BRASS INSTRUMENTS THAT'LL MAKE IT AWESOME, FOR SURE!
IT'S THANKS TO CHLOE.
WHAT A FAMILY!

DAD... I HAVEN'T HAD A CHANCE TO TELL YOU YET, BUT I'M SO HAPPY BEING HERE WITH YOU...

WITH YOU, AND ARTHUR, OF COURSE!

Now everything just needs the final touch...
DON'T MOVE AND BREATHE IN DEEP, JACKIE!
-›OOOF!‹-...
YOU'RE BEAUTIFUL, LOUANNE.
THANKS, COWBOY!
WHAT ABOUT THE YOUNG-STERS?
HOW WILL YOU DISGUISE YOURSELVES?
NONE OF THESE COSTUMES REALLY SUIT ME, I THINK--
DON'T COUNT ON ME PUTTING ON ONE OF THESE THINGS!
I'M JUST HERE TO HELP OUT.
SURPRISE! THESE WERE THE ONLY TWO STILL AVAILABLE.
IT'S THE ONLY CHOICE! THEY'LL LOOK AWESOME ON YOU.
YEAH...

The whole neighborhood is equally geared up...
MY OUTFIT IS SO COOL!
YOU HAVEN'T SEEN MINE. IT'S MAGNIFICENT!
?!

HAS THIS STORE BEEN TRENDING OR SOME-THING?
LET'S MAKE SURE.
IF THERE ARE ANY GOOD DEALS, WE MUSTN'T MISS OUT!

BUT... THERE'S NOTHING LEFT?
LOOKS LIKE WE MISSED OUT...

WHAT THE HECK? THEIR MARCH THING ISN'T CANCELED ANYMORE?!

NEIGHBORHOOD
CARNIVA
SUNDAY
COME ONE, COME AL
FAMILIES AND FRIEN
3:00 PM:
4:30 PM
I DON'T UNDERSTAND! MY MOM TOLD ME EVERYTHING HAD BEEN DEALT WITH...
THIS ISN'T RIGHT. WE HAVE TO TURN THEM IN!

YOUR MOM, YOUR MOM... YOUR MOM'S A LOSER! JUST LOOK, THIS RENDEZVOUS FOR FASHION DISASTERS HAS BECOME ***THE PLACE TO BE***.

WE NO LONGER HAVE ANY CHOICE! WE MUST BE THE STARS OF THAT PARTY!

MA'AM, WE NEED OUTFITS FOR THE CARNIVAL!
WE WANT UNIQUE COSTUMES, COSTUMES NOBODY'S EVER WORN BEFORE US.
I'M CERTAIN YOU HAVE ENOUGH TASTE TO MEET OUR EXPECTATIONS!
YOU'VE COME TOO LATE. I WAS ABOUT TO SHUT THE STORE.
EVERYTHING'S ALREADY BEEN SOLD, TOO...
THE CARNIVAL WILL BE A DISASTER WITHOUT OUR PRESENCE!
DO YOU KNOW WHAT ELEGANCE IS?!
YOU'LL BE RESPONSIBLE FOR A CRUSHING FAILURE!
UNLESS...
I MAY HAVE SOMETHING LEFT IN THE NEW LINE...
BUT I'M WARNING YOU, NOT EVERYBODY CAN PULL THEM OFF.
THAT'S PERFECT. WE'RE NOT EVERYBODY!

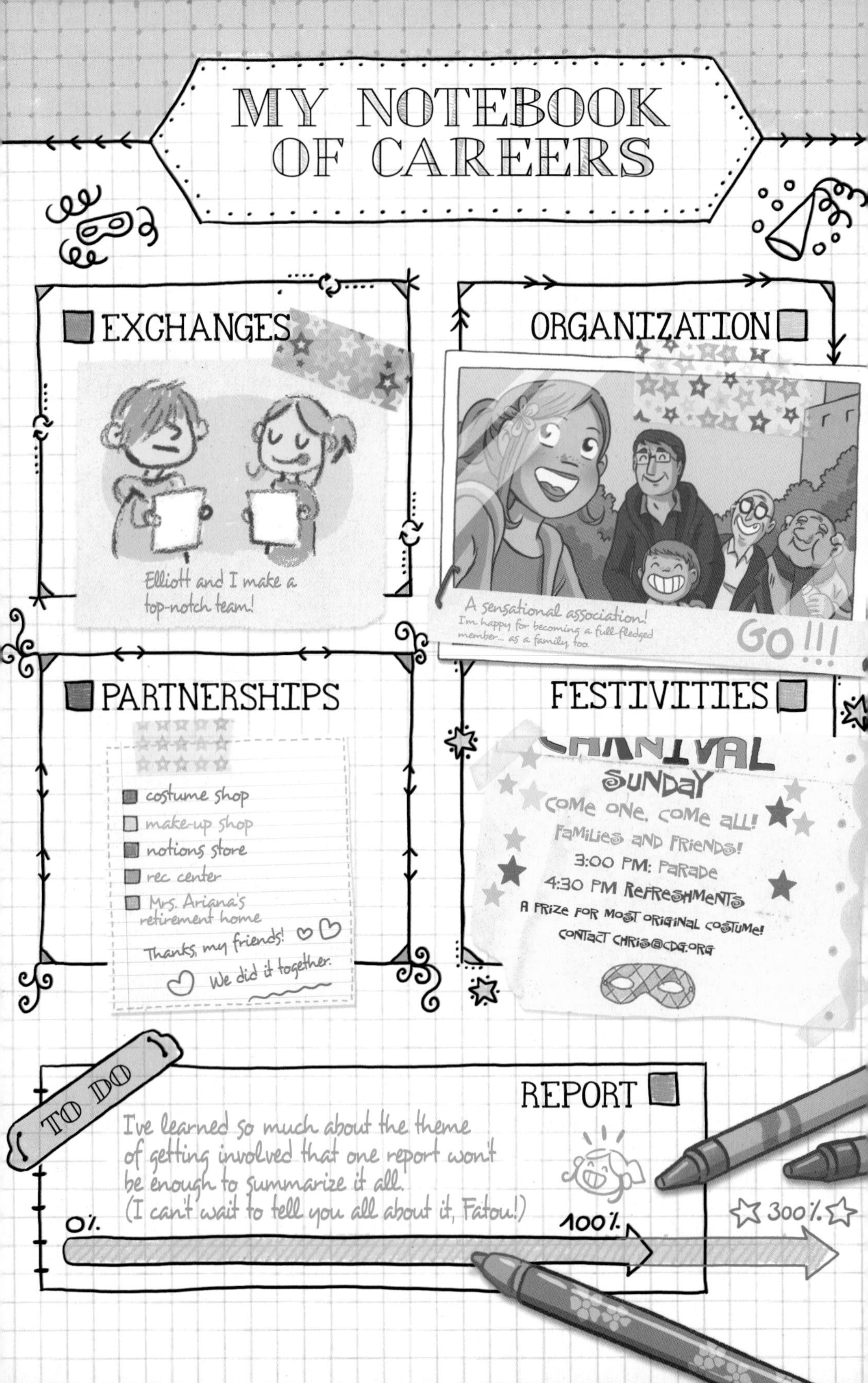

MY NOTEBOOK OF CAREERS
EXCHANGES
Elliott and I make a top-notch team!
ORGANIZATION
A sensational association!
I'm happy for becoming a full-fledged member... as a family, too.
GO!!!
PARTNERSHIPS
costume shop
make-up shop
notions store
rec center
Mrs. Ariana's retirement home
Thanks, my friends!
We did it together.
FESTIVITIES
SUNDAY
COME ONE, COME ALL!
FAMILIES AND FRIENDS!
3:00 PM: PARADE
4:30 PM REFRESHMENTS
A PRIZE FOR MOST ORIGINAL COSTUME!
CONTACT CHRIS@CDG.ORG
TO DO
REPORT
I've learned so much about the theme of getting involved that one report won't be enough to summarize it all.
(I can't wait to tell you all about it, Fatou!)
0%
100%
300%

MY FRIENDS, WE CAN BE PROUD OF OURSELVES. IN THE FACE OF ADVERSITY, WE WERE ABLE TO HELP ONE ANOTHER... MORE IMPORTANTLY, WE SHOWED WHO WE ARE. SO, LET THIS DAY BE THE BEGINNING OF A JOYFUL RENEWAL SIGNALING BEAUTIFUL PROJECTS!

FOR THE PRESIDENT, HIP HIP...

HOORAAAAY!
HA HA! TO INAUGURATE THIS RENEWAL, I ASK OUR KING AND OUR QUEEN OF THE DAY DO US THE HONOR OF OPENING THE PARADE.

HURRY UP, ELLIOTT. EVERYONE'S WAITING FOR US!
I DON'T LOOK TOO RIDICULOUS?

NO WAY! HERE WE GO, MILORD!

LET'S GET THIS PARTY STARTED!

CHLOE! CHLOE!
FATOU?! YOU MADE IT BACK IN TIME!

YOU'VE BECOME A QUEEN. NO WAY WAS I MISSING THAT!
AND WHERE DID YOU FIND THAT INCREDIBLE COSTUME?

A GIFT FROM MY AUNT LORRAINE. IT WAS PERFECT TIMING!

LOOK! IT'S THE FRUIT OF THE LOOM!
OR ARE THEY A FRUIT SALAD?
THEY LOOK SO GOOD, I'M GETTING HUNGRY HEE-HEE!

YOU KNOW WHAT? I'VE NEVER WANTED TO WORK ON A REPORT SO MUCH!

TEST

AMONG A GROUP OF FRIENDS, WHAT POSITION BEST FITS YOU?

1 When someone asks your opinion:

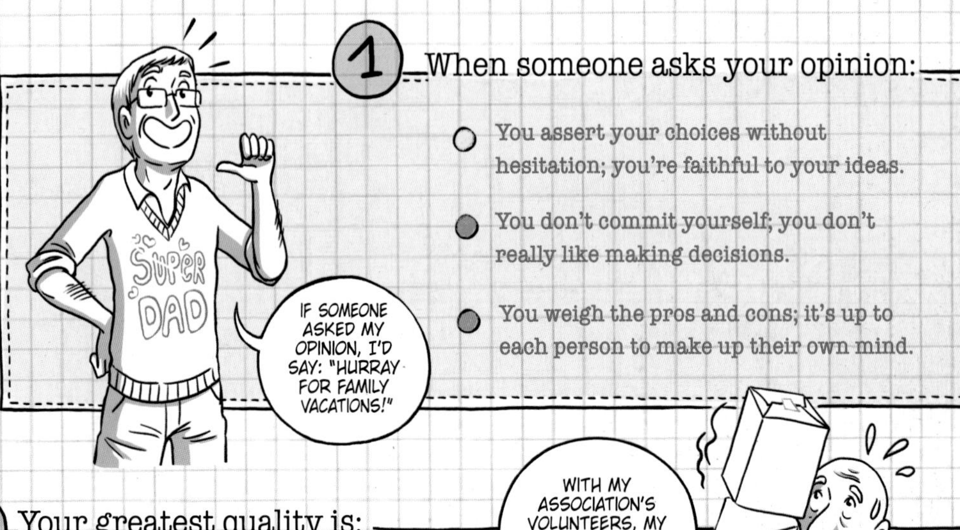

- You assert your choices without hesitation; you're faithful to your ideas.
- You don't commit yourself; you don't really like making decisions.
- You weigh the pros and cons; it's up to each person to make up their own mind.

2 Your greatest quality is:

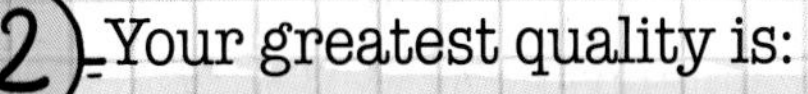

- Patience: good things come to those who wait.
- Determination: you never give up.
- Listening: you're always attentive.

3 Faced with a problem, you have a tendency to:

- Ask others what must be done; sometimes it's useful to have different opinions.
- Apply your own experience; you're always ready to give a hand.
- Take immediate action; you hate when things drag out.

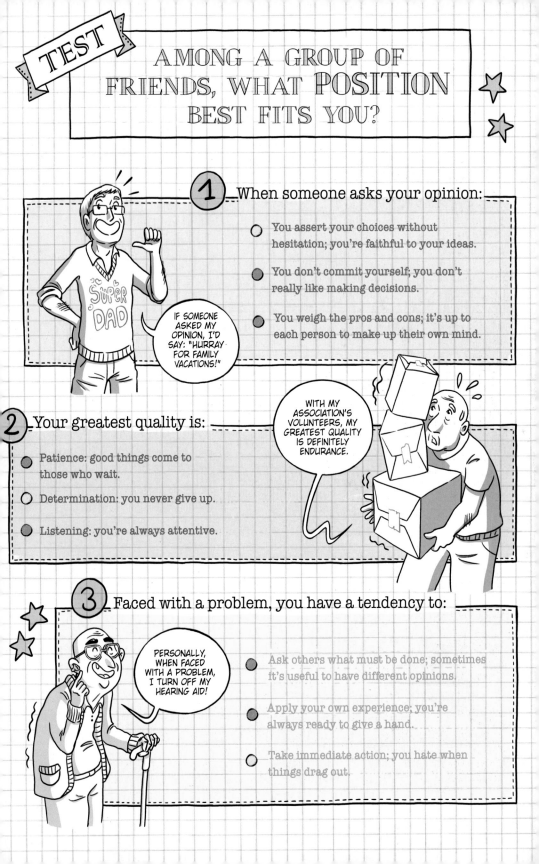

4 The costume that best matches your personality would likely be:

- ○ An adventurer; nothing scares you.
- ● A princess; you love being pampered.
- ● A lawyer; you're very talented at explaining things in detail.

I'M THE KING OF COWBOYS!

5 For you, helping out is:

- ● A priority; you need to get involved in causes.
- ○ Natural; becoming connected is habitual.
- ● Conceivable; you're waiting to find out more about the person involved.

WITH A BROTHER LIKE MINE, HELPING YOUR NEIGHBOR IS NEVER A SURE THING!

ANSWERS

You mostly have ○

There's always a leader in a group. And, without hesitation, that person would be you! You're a fighter, and like all fighters, you're endowed with an infectious enthusiasm, driving others to give the best of themselves. You're very responsive, you're not at all the sort to let a situation deteriorate. Just pay attention to staying as even-handed as possible. it's important to let everyone express themselves as best as they can.

You mostly have ●

Naturally reserved, you don't like drawing attention to yourself. Discreet and attentive, you prefer listening to others over putting yourself in the spotlight. In fact, your friends appreciate your restraint and tranquility! In a group, therefore, you'd be more of a follower. Don't be afraid, however, of asserting your opinion when you disagree, or else you risk seeming like a naïve person whom people can ask anything of or can get you to do everything out of an excess of kindness.

You mostly have ●

In a group, you definitely would occupy the place of the advisor! Very often, in fact, people turn to you spontaneously to confide in you. Disliking haste and always preferring to think before speaking and acting, you know how to guide others when they need it. Your opinion counts for your entourage, so don't forget that this trust is precious; take good care of it.

COME ON, LET'S GET MOTIVATED!
PFFF!... EVERYONE'S GOT THEIR OWN PACE, YOU KNOW!
IF YOU NEED ADVICE ON STRETCHING YOUR POCKET MONEY, CALL AUNT JACKIE!

Bonjour,
my friend!
I

NOTE:

Previously, in CHLOE #1-4 graphic novels, the location where Chloe and her family and friends have loved, lost, studied, fought, worked, and played was never specified. That is, until now. Chloe Blin and her family are French and live in a French suburb. In this story, when a new foreign exchange student comes from the United Kingdom, Chloe gets very self conscious about her English. That is because she speaks French. We at Charmz have translated it for readers to better follow along. In this story, when Chloe and friends are *actually* speaking English, their text will be in red to show they are speaking a foreign language. Likewise, when the English students are struggling with speaking a foreign language, their mistakes are shown in English, so some wording will be off. That is because they are actually struggling with French. The important thing about learning a language is practice, the friends you will make will not worry about how perfect your grammar is or how exact your conjugations are. Be like Chloe and dive into a new culture and language, you might just fall in love!

One Sunday evening in the BLIN family home...
TEEBEELEEEEET
CALL

I WONDER WHO COULD BE CALLING US AT THIS HOUR?
TEEBEELEEET
HELLO, HELLO... **CARTOON** SPEAKING!

YES?
OH, GOOD EVENING, **MRS. PANIGOT...**

DO YOU KNOW WHAT YOUR ENGLISH TEACHER WANTS WITH US, **MISTY** DEAR?
MMM, HMMM, MMM...

I UNDER-STAND.
I'LL CALL YOU RIGHT BACK.

THAT'S TERRIBLE!
CLIC

WHAT?
WHAT'S GOING ON?

HA, HA, HA! SORRY, I COULDN'T HELP MYSELF! YOU SHOULD'VE SEEN YOUR FACES...
VERY FUNNY, DAD.

DON'T WORRY; IT'S NOTHING SERIOUS. MRS. PANIGOT JUST WANTED TO ASK US IF WE'D HOST ONE OF THE NINTH GRADE BRITISH EXCHANGE STUDENTS.
THEIR HOME-ROOM TEACHER IS OUT SICK AND THEY STILL NEED A FEW REPLACEMENT HOST FAMILIES... IT WOULD BE FOR A WEEK.
OH, IF IT'S JUST THAT...

OF COURSE, WE'LL WELCOME HER HERE WITH US. WE CAN'T JUST LEAVE THE LITTLE GIRL OUT IN THE COLD.

RIGHT, CHLOE?
WELL YES, OF COURSE!

BESIDES, IT WILL BE A CHANCE TO WORK ON YOUR ENGLISH.
REDIAL

UHH...

Agitation

DRRIIIING
YOU'RE GOING TO HOST AN EXCHANGE STUDENT, TOO?

YES!
THATH THO COOL, ITHN'T IT?

WE'LL SEE...
YOU AREN'T HAPPY ABOUT THAT, CHLOE?

YES. IT COULD BE NICE, BUT I'M REALLY BAD AT FOREIGN LANGUAGES... WE'LL NEVER MANAGE TO UNDERSTAND EACH OTHER!

BESIDES, THEY HAVEN'T TOLD US ANYTHING ABOUT WHAT THE PERSON WE'RE HOSTING LIKES.

WELL--

HEY, *LAME-O*, THERE'S A REASON FOR THAT: YOU DON'T HAVE *ANY* TASTE. SO YOU WOULDN'T HAVE HAD ANYTHING IN COMMON ANYWAY!

AT LEAST OUR EXCHANGE STUDENTS ARE LUCKY.
THEY COULD'VE GOTTEN STUCK WITH CHLOE BLIN!

HAHAHA!
COME ON, IT'S TIME. WE'D BETTER HURRY.
LET'S GO SEE MRS. PANIGOT IN ENGLISH CLASS. I'M SURE SHE'LL HELP YOU FEEL BETTER.

But nothing goes as expected...
HEY THERE, CLASS 9B, WHAT ARE YOU STILL DOING IN THE HALL?

HELLO, KIDS!

SORRY I'M LATE, MIREILLE. I HAD A BIT OF A PROBLEM...

HMM... EXCUSE ME, MRS. PANIGOT. COULD WE HAVE SOME DETAILS ABOUT THE ENGLISH STUDENTS?
UNFORTUNATELY NOT!

MY ABSENT COLLEAGUE HAS ALL THEIR FILES WITH HER. ALL WE KNOW IS THAT THEY'RE YOUR AGE AND ARE IN YEAR TEN, WHICH IS THE EQUIVALENT OF 3RD IN OUR COUNTRY...
DO THEY THPEAK A LITTLE FRENTH?
AT LEATHT ATH WELL ATH YOU. HA HA HA!

QUIET, PLEASE. JUST BECAUSE YOU CHOSE NOT TO HOST A STUDENT, DOESN'T MEAN YOU SHOULD THINK YOU CAN DO ANYTHING YOU WANT, MISS ANISSA!
AS FOR YOU, MARK, DON'T WORRY. IT'S A LOT EASIER TO UNDERSTAND A FOREIGN LANGUAGE WHEN YOU'RE USING IT EVERY DAY.

SHE DIDN'T ANSWER OUR QUESTION AT ALL... WE STILL DON'T KNOW IF THEY KNOW ANY FRENCH.
DO YOU THINK YOU COULD TALK FOR ME SO I CAN COMMUNICATE WITH THEM, FATOU?
CHLOE'S GOING TO FAIL. SHE'S HOPELESS IN ENGLISH... CHLOE'S GOING TO FAIL...

The whole class is excited!
HELLO
Party

WE HAVE TO SHOW OUR NEW ENGLISH FRIENDS THAT WE'RE SUPER ORGANIZED IN FRANCE!

HOW DO YOU TRANSLATE, "BIENVENUE" AGAIN?
EASY, IT'S "WELCOME."

I COULDN'T REMEMBER EITHER... THIS IS AWFUL. I WON'T EVEN BE ABLE TO WELCOME THEM!

Positivity is important...
I HOPE MY EXCHANGE STUDENT WILL HAVE LOTS OF THINGS TO TEACH US ABOUT THEIR COUNTRY. WHAT DO YOU THINK YOURS WILL BE LIKE?
I DON'T CARE ATH LONG ATH THEY LIKE VIDEO GAMETH!

HOW ABOUT YOU, CHLOE?
HMMM... I HOPE SHE'S FUNNY AND THAT WE CAN UNDERSTAND EACH OTHER WELL.
WELCOME

THAT WOULD BE REALLY AWESOME... AND THAT'S HOW IT WILL BE, FATOU'S WORD!

At home, preparations are in full swing, too...

HOW WAS YOUR DAY, MISTY?

DID YOU LEARN MORE ABOUT YOUR EXCHANGE STUDENTS?
MMM.

NOTHING TO THESE ENGLISH DISHES!

DON'T MOVE, CARTOON. YOU'RE GOING TO BE SO HANDSOME!

FRENCH-ENGLISH DICTIONARY

WHAT WILL WE BE ABLE TO DO TOGETHER? MAYBE SHE'D LIKE TO RIDE BIKES? HOW DO YOU SAY THAT IN ENGLISH AGAIN?
WHAT A PAIN! I CAN'T REMEMBER. EVERYTHING'S SO COMPLICATED.
I HOPE SHE LIKES OUR HOUSE, AT LEAST...
FRENCH-ENGLISH DICTIONARY

* FRENCH FOR "PLEASED TO MEET YOU..."

CHIN UP, CHLOE...
HERE!

CHLOE BLIN, THIS IS *KATHLEEN WOOD*.
KATHLEEN WOOD, THIS IS CHLOE BLIN.

HELLO!

DO YOU LIKE VEUX-FIDÉO, *OLIFER*?
VIDEO GAMES, OH, YEAHHHH!
...
ARE YOU ALSO THE CLASS REP-RESENTATIVE, *LINDSAY*?
YES, THAT'S RIGHT! I'M THE CLASS REP IN ENGLAND.

BLEH. I'M ALREADY SICK OF HOW MY EXCHANGE STUDENT LOOKS. DID YOU SEE HER STYLE? I'M GOING TO DIE IF YOU PUT ME WITH HER!
?

HEE-HEE! LOOK, I HAVE TO ADMIT IT'S THE OPPOSITE FOR ME! THERE AREN'T ENOUGH PLACES IN THE BOYS' HOUSES... SO I'VE HIT THE JACKPOT! HE'S *TOO* CUTE!

SHALL WE GO, CHLOE? YOUR PARENTS ARE WAITING...

YES, HE'S A GREAT MUSICIAN!
BVVRRRRRR

HE HAS A GOOD VOICE AND HE PLAYS THE GUITAR REALLY WELL, TOO.
SURE!

IT'S CRAZY... SHE ISN'T SAYING A THING TO ME, BUT SHE'S TALKING NONSTOP WITH MY UNCLE!

ALL BECAUSE I'M JUST HOPELESS AT ENGLISH. ANISSA WAS RIGHT....

HELLO, KATHLEEN! WE'VE REALLY BEEN LOOKING FORWARD TO MEETING YOU.
COME ON IN!

THAT'S WONDERFUL!

HERE'S WHERE YOU'LL SLEEP, WITH CHLOE.
CLIC
OH, OKAY...

THANK YOU.

UH...WE SAID SHE'D GET THE SPARE MATTRESS, RIGHT?
IT DOESN'T MATTER, HONEY. WHAT'S MOST IMPORTANT IS FOR YOUR EXCHANGE STUDENT TO FEEL AS IF SHE'S IN HER OWN HOME HERE. BESIDES, IT'S ONLY FOR A SHORT WEEK...

Communication continues to be complicated....

MEOW!

COME ON, CAT!
UHMM... UHMM... SEE, KATHLEEN, MY CAT HAS AN ENGLISH NAME. HE'S CALLED, "CARTOON!"
THAT MEANS "DESSIN ANIMÉ." BUT WELL, HE'S A "CHAT" IN FRENCH.

EVEN IF HE REALLY SPEAKS IN CAT TONGUE!
?

LIKE A CAT TONGUE... THE COOKIE! HA HA! DO YOU GET IT?
OH, GEEZ. I CAN'T EVEN EXPRESS MYSELF PROPERLY IN FRENCH...

CLIC

Still, everyone tries very hard!

WHAT A BEAUTIFUL DRESS, KATHLEEN!

THAT VICTORIAN STYLE LOOKS GREAT ON YOU.
BUT DON'T YOU HAVE TO WEAR YOUR SCHOOL UNIFORM TO GO TO SCHOOL?
YES, UNIFORM REQUIRED IN SCHOOLS ENGLISH. BUT HERE, IT'S OKAY!

SHE SPEAKS A LITTLE FRENCH, ACTUALLY. BUT STILL NOT WITH ME. PFFF!
OF COURSE, UH... VICTORIAN... STYLE!
GOOD. HAVE A SEAT, YOUNG LADY! I MADE AN ENGLISH BREAKFAST JUST FOR YOU.

NO BACON, HOWEVER. I COULDN'T FIND ANY... BUT I'VE GOT TURKEY BREAST, AND INSTEAD OF KIDNEY BEANS, I GOT US WHITE BEANS. TELL ME WHAT YOU THINK, KATHLEEN!

COME ON, COME ON, START EATING!

WE HAVE TO TEMPT KATHLEEN. SHE'S TOO SHY.

OH, OH, THANK YOU. VERY GOOD... JUST NOT HUNGRY THIS MORNING...

Going back to school doesn't make things better...
LIBRARY

STUDENTS, I HOPE THE FIRST EVENING SPENT WITH YOUR EXCHANGE STUDENTS WAS A SUCCESS.

GOOD MORNING, GUYS!
HELLO, ETHAN.
HI!
LESLIE'S SO LUCKY... HER EXCHANGE STUDENT SEEMS NICE...

BEFORE STARTING TODAY'S LESSON, LET ME TAKE THIS OPPORTUNITY TO REMIND YOU TO FILL OUT YOUR FACT SHEETS ABOUT ENGLAND. IT'S IMPORTANT TO KEEP LEARNING MORE ABOUT YOUR GUESTS.
DON'T WANDER OFF, ETHAN! YOUR PLACE IS AT MY SIDE.

WELL! LADIES AND GENTLEMEN... THE LIBRARIAN, MRS. TILLETT, WAS KIND ENOUGH TO INVITE US INTO HER LIBRARY FOR A LITTLE FRENCH-ENGLISH VOCABULARY COMPETITION...

AHEM!
PWAH!
THIS WHOLE DAY STILL ISN'T GOING TO BE EASY!

THE WINNERS WILL GET THESE "BANDES DESSINÉES," WHICH ARE CALLED "COMICS," BY OUR BRITISH AND AMERICAN NEIGHBORS.

OH, YEAH!

The contest is going full tilt!
LAST QUESTION!
IN FRANCE, WE SOMETIMES USE THE EXPRESSION, "AVOIR UN CHAT DANS LA GORGE," FOR WHEN YOU'RE HOARSE.
IN ENGLAND, YOU HAVE THE SAME EXPRESSION, BUT WITH A DIFFERENT KIND OF ANIMAL. WHICH ONE IS IT?
READING CLUB

GOT IT?
NO IDEA...
OH, YES!
DO YOU KNOW THE ANSWER?
...

F...RO...
FROG!

IT'S A FROG, MA'AM!

GOOD ANSWER. THE EXPRESSION IS, "TO HAVE A FROG IN YOUR THROAT."

THEY'RE REALLY LUCKY TO BE ABLE TO UNDERSTAND EACH OTHER SO EASILY...
YOU ARE THE BEST!

Communication certainly seem to have broken down between Chloe and Kathleen.
NOT TOO CROWDED IN HERE? IT'S NOT EVERY DAY THAT WE HAVE BRITISH STUDENTS IN GEOGRAPHY...

ACTUALLY, I CAN'T REMEMBER THE NAME OF THIS COUNTRY IN ENGLISH! COULD SOMEONE HELP ME?

ME, ME!

POKE
GO ON... YOU KNOW THE ANSWER!

OUCH!

SOR... SORRY...
?

IS SOMETHING WRONG WITH KATHLEEN?
NO, IT'S NOTHING.

THEY'RE A GREAT MATCH. BOTH ARE REAL DIMWITS... I LOVE IT! HA, HA, HA!
STAR

DON'T WORRY. SHE HAS TO BE FEELING A LITTLE SHY. I'M SURE IT'LL WORK OUT.
MHHH...

Some clarification would be welcome!

AND HERE WE GO AGAIN...

GRRR. THIS DESSERT RECIPE SHOULDN'T BE VERY DIFFICULT!

KATHLEEN ALREADY WENT UP TO YOUR ROOM? BUT SHE HAD LOTS OF ENERGY YESTERDAY...
BACK WHERE SHE'S FROM, CLASSES END EARLY, AROUND 3 OR 4 P.M. MAYBE SHE'S TIRED.

PFFF! KATHLEEN HERE, KATHLEEN THERE...

IS THERE A PROBLEM WITH YOUR EXCHANGE STUDENT, CHLOE?
IT'S JUST THAT... THAT I NO LONGER EXIST SINCE SHE CAME HERE.

PLUS SHE REFUSES TO SAY A WORD TO ME BECAUSE I'M SO BAD AT ENGLISH.
NO ONE CARES HOW I FEEL BECAUSE IT'S MY OWN FAULT THAT I'M SO LAME.

CALM DOWN, MISTY. WE DIDN'T REALIZE THE SITUATION WAS SO DIFFICULT.

YOUR UNCLE WAS JUST ASKING WHAT WAS NEW, SWEETIE! EVEN IF WE ASK HOW KATHLEEN'S DOING, THAT DOESN'T MEAN SHE'S REPLACED YOU HERE.
IT'S NORMAL TO CONSIDER HER BEFORE YOU BECAUSE SHE'S THE GUEST WHO'S IN A PLACE SHE DOESN'T KNOW, WITH PEOPLE WHO ARE STRANGERS TO HER.

BUT NO ONE KNEW YOU WEREN'T GETTING ALONG WITH EACH OTHER.
I DIDN'T KNOW HOW TO TELL YOU. PLUS EVERY-THING WAS GOING OKAY WITH YOU...

BUT I CAN'T MANAGE TO COMMUNICATE WITH HER. IT'S AS IF THE WORDS GET STUCK. AND NOW SHE CAN'T STAND ME!
ACTUALLY, I WOULD REACT THE WAY SHE IS IF I WERE IN HER PLACE.

JUST BREATHE. HOW WELL YOU SPEAK ENGLISH DOESN'T MATTER. IT'S A LIVING LANGUAGE; IT'S SPOKEN! THERE'S NO SHAME EVER.

JUST A WORD TO THE WISE: LISTEN TO YOUR FEELINGS AND REACH OUT TOWARDS OTHERS... IF YOU LET YOURSELF DISCOVER, EVERYTHING WILL GO WELL. YOU FOLLOW ME?
O...OKAY. I'LL TRY!

BLASTED RECIPES!
HEEHEE
HAHAHA

Last name: Blin
First name: Chloe
Class: 9B

Fact sheet England

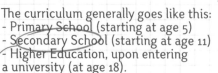

UNITED KINGDOM

Scotland
Northern Ireland
Ireland
Wales
England
London

??
?

I don't know where your town is, Kathleen. I definitely don't know anything about you. ('n')

Geography

The United Kingdom is an island nation in the northwest of Europe. it consists of England, Scotland, Wales, and Northern Ireland.
Its capital is London.

Flag

The flag of the United Kingdom is called the Union Jack. It combines the cross of St. George from the English flag with the cross of St. Andrew from the Scottish flag and of St. Patrick, to represent Ireland.

ARGH!
I can't even remember if the cross on the flag is
- RED?
- BLUE?
(How embarrassing!)

Language

Historically, English has been the language of the United Kingdom, but it's also become the language for international communication, used in diplomacy, trade, and also on the internet.

There really are so many people who can speak this language... Why can't I?

Driving

In England, as in several other countries, such as Japan, India, and also South Africa, they drive on the left!
However, among the European nations, vehicles almost always drive on the right. Only Great Britain and Ireland stand apart in this.

Do I have to stand apart because I'm a leftie?

School system

The curriculum generally goes like this:
- Primary School (starting at age 5)
- Secondary School (starting at age 11)
- Higher Education, upon entering a university (at age 18).

in theory, 3rd level should fit in here.

Reflection

The day of the school trip arrives.
HEY, LOOK WHAT OLIVER LENT ME! A GAME NOT YET RELEATHED IN FRANTH! WANT TO TRY IT?
NO, THANKS, MARK. LINDSAY AND I WERE PLANNING TO USE THE TRIP TO FINISH OUR FACT SHEETS...

UH... DO YOU WANT... TO SIT NEXT TO ME, KATHLEEN?

I'M REALLY NOT GOOD IN ENGLISH, SORRY...

OH, NO! WHAT'S *SHE* DOING HERE?

I THOUGHT THIS WAS ONLY FOR THE EXCHANGE STUDENTS?
THERE ARE PROBABLY A FEW PLACES LEFT. HER PARENTS PROBABLY PUSHED TO SIGN HER UP ANYWAY.

SO, ARE YOU HAPPY, CHLOE?

DON'T STAY NEXT TO HER. YOU CAN CLEARLY SEE SHE'S STILL LEAVING YOU ALONE! SHE DOESN'T CARE ABOUT YOU! SHE BARELY TALKS TO YOU...

QUIET BACK THERE!
I'M ASKING YOU TO STOP THAT!

DON'T LISTEN TO ANISSA. SHE ONLY SAYS NASTY THINGS...

SHE ALWAYS WANTS TO CREATE PROBLEMS. BUT IF SHE'S JEALOUS OF US, THAT MEANS SHE'S ALSO AFRAID THE TWO OF US WILL BECOME FRIENDS... YOU UNDERSTAND, RIGHT?

COULD YOU MOVE, LESLIE, DEAR? I NEED TO SIT NEXT TO THE WINDOW SO I DON'T GET SICK.
WELL...

THAT'S TRUE. CHLOE'S RIGHT. SHE'S A BAD GIRL.
SHE'TH REALLY POITHON!

POI... THON? WHAT'S THAT?

I CAN TRANSLATE THAT... IN MARK LANGUAGE, THAT MEANS, "POISON."
HEE-HEE!

The tour starts right on time...
Museum of Popular Traditions
YOU SHOULD BE AWARE THAT BEFORE BECOMING A MONITOR, I WAS A GUIDE FIRST.
OH, YEAH!
?

SO I'LL SEE TO IT MYSELF THAT YOU'LL APPRECIATE THIS MAGNIFICENT MUSEUM OF POPULAR TRADITIONS.
entrance

MUSEUM OF DUSTY ARTS, MOSTLY!
HAHA
LOOK, THERE'S NAOMIE'S EXCHANGE STUDENT IN THE DISPLAY CASE!

HA, HA, HA! TOTALLY! AND WE CAN BADMOUTH HER AS MUCH AS WE WANT, SINCE SHE DOESN'T UNDERSTAND ANYTHING.
WHERE'S ETHAN? IS THAT HOW YOU KEEP AN EYE ON YOUR EXCHANGE STUDENT, LESLIE?
FIND HIM RIGHT NOW!

HEY, CASSIE! YOU CAN TOUR WITH US IF YOU'D LIKE INSTEAD OF WITH THOSE THREE PAINS...

THEY'RE POITHON!
HEE-HEE!

YOU TWO ARE LUCKY TO BE EACH OTHER'S EXCHANGE STUDENT.

TWENTY MINUTES FREE TIME IN THE OLD TOWN.

WE'LL MEET AT THE FOOT OF THE GALLIC-ROMAN TOWER...
ARE YOU SURE THAT TOWER'S SO "ANCIENT?"

GRRR!... THAT'S WHAT I SAID!

I'LL BE RIGHT BACK! I JUST WANT TO SEE SOMETHING OVER THERE...

WHY IS HE HIDING LIKE THAT?

SHOOT! WHERE'D HE GO?

PSSSSTTT!

SORRY IF I SCARED YOU!
I JUST TO WANT TO ADMIRE IT IN PEACE AND QUIET. I'VE HAD IT WITH MY EXCHANGE STUDENT AND HER FRIENDS-- THEY'RE ALL CRAZY...
WOW, YOU REALLY SPEAK FRENCH WELL!

THANKS! OFTEN HAVE COME TO FRANCE ON VACATION WITH MY PARENTS IN BRITAIN... UH BRITTANY. DO YOU KNOW BRITTANY?
TOTALLY! THAT'S WHERE MY GRANNY ANGELA LIVES, RIGHT BY THE SEA.

YOU AND ME MAY HAVE BUMPED INTO EACH OTHER ALREADY WITHOUT KNOWING IT. HA HA!

IT WOULD BE SO EASY IF MY EXCHANGE STUDENT SPOKE FRENCH LIKE YOU...
WE'VE ONLY MANAGED TO EXCHANGE A FEW WORDS TODAY, EVEN THOUGH WE DON'T REALLY KNOW EACH OTHER YET.

KATHLEEN SHY. SHE SENT MESSAGES IN THE EVENING BECAUSE NOTHING TO UNDERSTAND THAT YOU WERE SAYING TO HER IN FRENCH. SHE THOUGHT YOU WERE MAKING FUN OF HER...

NO, EXACTLY THE OPPOSITE!
YOU'RE SUPER NICE. MAYBE YOU COULD SUGGEST SOME THINGS SHE'S COMFORTABLE WITH, EVEN WITHOUT TALKING MUCH... LIKE THIS NICE WALK!

THANKS FOR THE ADVICE, ETHAN!
GOOD LUCK WITH ANISSA, NAOMIE, AND LESLIE BECAUSE THEY'RE ALWAYS PUSHY. MAYBE TRY FOCUSING ON LESLIE, FOR STARTERS. SHE'S THE ONE YOU'LL SEE MOST OFTEN.

COULD WE BE FRIENDS?
OF COURSE! BY THE WAY... MY NAME IS CHLOE.
NICE TO MEET YOU, CHLOE!

WHAT DO YOU THINK OF THIS OUTFIT?
PRETTY HARD TO WEAR TO SCHOOL!
HMMM, A LITTLE STRANGE...
AND WHAT ABOUT THIS?
SIR, YES, SIR!

DO YOU WANT TO TRY?

The weekend should be for resting...
HUH, YOU'RE LEAVING WITHOUT HAVING BREAKFAST?
NO, NO THANKS, DAD! I'M GOING FOR A WALK WITH KATHLEEN. WE'LL GET SOMETHING IN TOWN. I ABSOLUTELY MUST SHOW HER A STORE.

OKAY, THAT LEAVES ALL THE MORE FOR US, HUH?

THERE IT IS! COME ON, LET'S GO IN!

YOU LIKE HUH?... DO YOU... UH... LIKE IT?

IT'S MAGIC!

THANK YOU, CHLOE.
THAT ISN'T ALL. LOOK!

THERE ARE LOTS OF THINGS IN YOUR STYLE...

EVEN MOVIES...
OR MUSICAL COMEDIES.

HELLO, YOUNG LADIES!

YOU SEEM GREATLY INTERESTED IN ALL THIS. IF YOU'RE ALSO FANS OF CERTAIN WORLDS, LIKE ME, WE'RE GOING TO BE SHOWING *MARY POPPINS* AND *OLIVER TWIST* IN A FEW MINUTES!
IT WILL BE IN THE MOVIE THEATRE THAT'S RIGHT WITHIN THE STORE.
OH, BUT THE SCREENING WILL BE THE ORIGINAL ENGLISH VERSION, WITH FRENCH SUBTITLES. WILL THAT BE OKAY WITH YOU, I HOPE?

PERFECT!

THAT WAS SO GREAT!

HOW DO YOU SAY, "GENIAL" IN ENGLISH?
"WONDERFUL!"
WELL, THAT'S GREAT NEWS...

AND THAT'S NOT THE ONLY THING, RIGHT *ANTHONY*?
OW... UH... YES... UH... THE DAY ISN'T ACTUALLY OVER YET. WE HAVE A SURPRISE FOR YOU, ALSO!

WHAT IS IT? WHAT IS IT?
IF WE TOLD YOU, IT WOULDN'T BE A SURPRISE, CHLOE.

THEORETICALLY, IT'S A PRESENT THAT EVERYONE REALLY NEEDS.
OKAY, OKAY, GET READY TO LEAVE IN 15 MINUTES!

TONIGHT, IT'S YOU... UH... YOU WHO'LL TRY ON MY DRESSES.

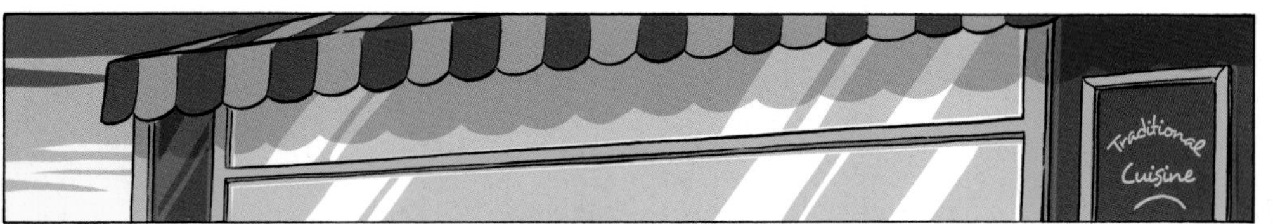
Traditional
Cuisine

YUM, IT'S SUPER HARD TO CHOOSE!
menu

HONEY, A LITTLE EXPLANATION PERHAPS... OF WHY WE'RE HERE TONIGHT?
DING DING

YES... SO... ACTUALLY, KATHLEEN, IT TURNS OUT... THAT MY ATTEMPTS AT ENGLISH CUISINE WEREN'T ALWAYS TOTALLY "SUCCESSFUL." SO WE FIGURED THE BEST THING WOULD BE TO SHOW YOU FRENCH CUISINE IN A RESTAURANT.
menu

BESIDES YOU MAY WELL IMAGINE THAT I COULD WHIP UP THESE DISHES AT HOME. I JUST NEED TO LOOK FOR THE RECIPES AND--

NO, NO, NO, STOP!
YOU NEED TO REST, SWEETHEART.

MMM, SMELLS GOOD...
IT'S DELICIOUS. TASTE IT!

MM YES, OKAY, OKAY. IT DOESN'T SEEM SO BAD.
SNIF SNIF

I KNOW SOMEONE WHO'LL BE MORE THAN A LITTLE JEALOUS, RIGHT?

The next day is just as busy...
LOOK, CHLOE! ETHAN'S BOWLING WITH LESLIE.

WHY DID HE TELL YOU? DO YOU LIKE BOWLING?

OH, NO, NO. NEVER DONE!
BUT MAYBE HE WOULD LIKE BETTER COMPANY...

WHAT A MAG-NI-FI-CENT IDEA, BOWLING!

I'M AN EXPERT AT IT!

I CAN'T WAIT TO SHOW YOU MY SPECIAL THROW!
DADDY, CHAMPION OF THE WORLD!

BOWLING

I DON'T UNDERSTAND. I'M USUALLY SO MUCH BETTER!
RATS, WE GOT HERE TOO LATE.
TOO LATE FOR WHAT? THE TOURNAMENT'S JUST BEGUN, MY DAUGHTER.

NO PROBLEM, YOU'LL SEE. IT'S SUPER SIMPLE. YOU JUST NEED TO...
PFFFF

LET THE MASTER DO IT! KATHLEEN, HERE'S WHAT YOU CAN ONE DAY ACHIEVE WITH A BIT OF EXPERIENCE...
SMAC

GO, DADDY!
!
MY TURN! MY TURN!
BING
NICE JOB, ARTHUR! THAT'S HOW IT'S REALLY PLAYED!

The two friends find their voices...
THAT'S IT. KATHLEEN, HAVE YOU FINISHED YOUR LIST OF WHAT YOU LIKE AND DON'T LIKE?
MMM... YES!
- friendship
- Nice people
- Cats
cats
spiders
IT'S AMAZING! WE'VE GOT LOTS OF THINGS IN COMMON.
WE LIKE HONESTY AND KINDNESS... THAT'S US, ISN'T IT?
EXACTLY.
CHLOE, YOU'RE A REALLY SUPER EXCHANGE STUDENT!
YOU, TOO, KATHLEEN! EVEN IF WE DON'T LIVE IN THE SAME COUNTRY, WE'RE A LOT ALIKE.
PLUS WE LOVE CATS, TOO!
HEE-HEE-HEE!

HEY, DO YOU REALLY THINK ETHAN TALKED TO YOU ABOUT BOWLING SO HE COULD SEE ME?
YES, SURE!
YOU REALLY LIKE HIM...

NO WAY!

WELL, I DON'T KNOW...
IT'S BEEN A LONG TIME SINCE I'VE FELT SO COMFORTABLE WITH A BOY, WITHOUT THINKING ABOUT IT.

YOU DON'T HAVE A BOYFRIEND?
NOT AT THE MOMENT.

I HAD A MAJOR RELATIONSHIP WITH A BOY NAMED ALEX, BUT HE MOVED TO ITALY. SINCE THEN EVERYTHING'S BEEN COMPLICATED. THERE'S ANOTHER BOY AT SCHOOL THAT I THINK I LIKE, BUT...
HOW ABOUT YOU, KATHLEEN?
ME LIKE YOU... IT'S COMPLICATED!

ANYWAY, ALL I KNOW IS THAT I'D REALLY LIKE TO SEE ETHAN AGAIN!
LOVE, LOVE, LOVE!

Last name: Blin/Wood
First name: Chloe/Kathleen
Class: 9B/9th Grade

Fact sheet England

n°2

Cuisine

-A **full English breakfast** always contains sausages, bacon, eggs, beans, tomatoes, and mushrooms. It's all served with toast, brown sauce, and tea with milk.

-**Fish and chips** is a fast food dish that consists of fish deep fried in batter or breadcrumbs and served with fries.

YUM

There are some good English dishes! (They're different from Dad's versions...)

Culture

England is famous throughout the world for its poetry, theatre, painting, and movies. Plus, all the permanent collections at the museums in the country are free, thanks to a system of optional donations, by which visitors give what they can/want.

TOO COOL!
Will the Museum of Popular Arts and Traditions be free soon?

Museum of Popular Traditions
-ADMIT ONE-

Fashion

Classic English fashion—"British fashion"—has been around since the 19th century.
New British fashion today is characterized by its great originality and spirit of innovation...

So cool

We're the new generation!

Leisure

The English invented lots of sports:
Cricket, tennis, darts, rugby, soccer...
And bowling? No! Bowling is American!

Pets

Cats often live in British houses. But even though the Siamese breed of cats originally came from Thailand, England is the first place they were seen outside their Asian birthplace, in 1884, when the British Consul General to Bangkok, Edward Blencowe Gould, brought back a couple of Siamese cats for his sister, Mrs. Veley.

Now I understand better why you like Cartoon, Kathleen!
(Hee-hee!)

Integration

Monday arrives, and our young heroine has just one thought in mind...
THERE THEY ARE!

HI, CHLOE! HELLO, KATHLEEN! LINDSAY AND I THOUGHT OF SOMETHING...
WE'D LIKE TO ARRANGE SOMETHING SPECIAL FOR THE EXCHANGE STUDENTS' DEPARTURE. HOW WOULD YOU LIKE TO HELP US PLAN?

TOTALLY! WE JUST, UH... FIRST NEED TO DO SOMETHING URGENT IN THE COURTYARD.

?
WE'LL BE RIGHT BACK!

CHLOE IS IN LOVE!

PSSST! THEY ARE NOT AROUND?

HEE-HEE! NO, IT'S GOOD. YOU CAN COME OUT.

SO, HOW WAS YOUR WEEKEND? IT DIDN'T LOOK EASY YESTERDAY AT THE BOWLING ALLEY...
YES, LESLIE NICE BUT SHE AND ME, NOTHING IN COMMON. THEN ANISSA ARRIVING AND I THINK LESLIE WAS SAD.

MMM... ANISSA DIDN'T STICK TOO MUCH TO YOU, AT LEAST?

OH, NO! I TOOK ADVANTAGE OF THE OPPORTUNITY TO TELL THEM I DIDN'T FEEL GOOD AND I LET THE GIRLS HANG OUT TOGETHER...

TO HELP YOU FORGET ALL THAT, WOULD YOU BE TEMPTED TO HELP OUR GROUP PUT TOGETHER A FAREWELL PARTY FOR YOU?

IT WOULD BE A CHANCE TO GET RID OF ANISSA, SINCE SHE DOESN'T HAVE AN EXCHANGE STUDENT...
YES, WITH PLEASURE, MISS!

KATHLEEN'S THE QUEEN OF ORGANIZING SHOWS IN OUR CLASS, RIGHT, KATH?

HOW ABOUT ENGLISH KARAOKE, TO OPEN OUR HEARTS MUSICALLY?

WE COULD MAKE SURE IT'S BILINGUAL WITH MIXED FRENCH-ENGLISH TEAMS.
THAT WAY, NO HANG-UPS FOR ANYONE!

GREAT!
COME ON, LET'S TELL THE OTHERS RIGHT AWAY!

I'M SINGIN' IN THE RAIN, JUST SINGIN' IN THE RAIN...

Everything goes smoothly...
BIENVENUE, WELCOME, BOYS AND GIRLS, TO THE COMMITTEE MEETING!
UH...HA, HA... I SEE YOU'RE ALREADY STARTED. THAT'S EXCELLENT!

SO, UH... WOULD SOMEONE LIKE TO SUGGEST SOME ENTERTAINMENT TO GO WITH THE FAREWELL SNACKS?

WE WOULD, MA'AM!

TAKE NOTES. WE NEED TO TELL ANISSA EVERYTHING!
YES, WELL, SHE JUST SHOULD'VE HAD AN EXCHANGE STUDENT, YOU KNOW? I'M SICK OF HER TAKING EVERYTHING OF MINE.

WE GOT TOGETHER IN A LITTLE GROUP AND WE WANT TO DO KARAOKE!
IN FRENCH AND ENGLISH.

INTERESTING... DO YOU HAVE ANY SPECIFIC IDEAS ABOUT HOW YOU'LL ORGANIZE IT?

LOTS! ETHAN HAS A REALLY NICE VOICE.
HE COULD START THE FIRST SONG TO GET EVERYONE GOING.
KATHLEEN WOULD BE OUR DECORATOR...
AND FATOUMATA WOULD BE OUR MC IN THE TWO LANGUAGES!

BRAVO, GOOD JOB! IN FACT, IT WOULD BE GOOD TO SET UP FRENCH-ENGLISH STUDENT TEAMS, WHICH WOULD BE A WONDERFUL MESSAGE.

HMMM, SO THAT THE PERFORMANCE IS PLEASANT TO LISTEN TO, MAYBE WE SHOULD MAKE SURE THE FIRST TEAM IS GOOD ENOUGH...
WHO AMONG YOU STUDENTS CAN SING AND ACCOMPANY ETHAN?

ME!
ME!
DON'T YOU START IN, TOO!

WE'LL HOLD AUDITIONS FOR VOLUNTEERS, WITH THE STUDENTS WHO THOUGHT UP THE PROJECT LEADING. THAT WAY THERE WON'T BE ANY PROBLEMS.
MEETING ADJOURNED.

CHLOE, WAIT!

WOULD YOU BE MY SINGING PARTNER?

SORRY, ETHAN, I WOULD REALLY HAVE LOVED TO, BUT I'M NOT VERY GOOD AT SINGING.

IN SHORT, THERE'S NO CHANCE I'LL BE CHOSEN.

The tension reaches its climax...
LIBRARY
Audition 5 p.m.

CHECK OUT THIS LINE FOR A SIMPLE DUO WITH ETHAN...
WHILE THAT ENGLISH IDIOT HAS NO TASTE AT ALL, OR ELSE HE WOULD HAVE SEIZED HIS CHANCE WITH ME LONG AGO!

SEE, I WASN'T LYING! SHE'S PRACTICING FOR THE AUDITION.
WHO DOES SHE THINK SHE IS?
I'M A SINGLE LADY, I'M A SINGLE LADY...

OH, IT'S YOU, ANISSA!

I TOLD HER THIS WAS MY TURF. I THOUGHT THAT WAS CLEAR!
POC
HEY!
LISTEN UP, AND I'M TELLING YOU LOUD AND CLEAR, ETHAN'S FOR ME. YOUR TAKING PART IN THIS LOUSY AUDITION IS OUT OF THE QUESTION!

ANYWAY, YOU CAN'T TRY OUT FOR IT, EITHER. THE PARTY'S ONLY FOR STUDENTS WHO HAVE EXCHANGE STUDENTS. BUT YOU WON'T MISS MUCH, DON'T WORRY.
OF COURSE, I WON'T MISS ANYTHING, SINCE I'LL BE THERE!
THIS SHOW DREADFULLY NEEDS A HEADLINER.
SO THAT WILL BE HOW I'LL SEDUCE THAT ENGLISH BOY THEN... MAYBE I'LL EVEN LET HIM KISS ME!

It seems like anything goes...
BUT...
THERE'S NO "BUT" THAT COUNTS. WHO'S IN CHARGE HERE? ENJOY MY TALENT INSTEAD! HA, HA, HA!

YOU SAY ONE WORD AND I'LL DESTROY YOU.
I'M GIVING YOU THREE SECONDS TO GET OUT OF HERE... ONE...
TWO...
THREE!

THE AUDITIONS ARE NOW OPEN.

WELL, I WOULD HAVE THOUGHT THERE'D BE MORE PEOPLE TRYING OUT FOR THE DUET WITH ETHAN, BUT SINCE THERE'S NO ONE EXCEPT YOU AFTER ALL, ANISSA, THE SPOT GOES RIGHT TO YOU.

THAT'S IMPOSSIBLE! THERE WERE LOTS OF APPLICANTS JUST NOW.
LET'S GO SEE WHAT'S GOING ON...

ENOUGH WASTING TIME! HERE, ANISSA, THESE ARE THE WORDS TO THE OPENING SONG. THERE WILL BE A SCREEN, BUT YOU SHOULD MASTER THEM.

NO WORRIES. I WON'T EVEN NEED THEM! SEE YOU AGAIN ON THE BIG DAY.

The situation demands some explanations...
HOW WATH IT THAT ANITHA WATH THE ONLY ONE WHO WATH AT THE AUDITIONTH?!
SOMETHING WEIRD'S GOING ON.
WAIT FOR ME HERE. I KNOW MANY OF THE STUDENTS WHO SIGNED UP. WE'LL GET OUR ANSWER...

IT'S EXACTLY WHAT I WAS AFRAID OF! ANISSA SCARED THEM ALL AWAY BY THREATENING THEM.

THAT PAIN GOT WHAT SHE WANTED. MRS. ROBINSON WON'T CHANGE IT...

THATH PATHETIC!
IT'S CHEATING!

IF ANISSA CHEATS, SHE'S NOT WORTHY OF THE PART! LET'S CHANGE THE SONG. WE'LL WAIT UNTIL A LITTLE BEFORE TO ALERT ANOTHER SINGER OF OUR SECRET. BUT WE'LL CHANGE THE SONG.
YES OR NO?

YES!

Time to practice...
DOOOO...

WELL, IT'S REALLY SWEET OF YOU TO SUGGEST THIS TO ME, KATHLEEN. BUT I DON'T THINK THESE SINGING EXERCISES WILL LET ME HELP ETHAN PRACTICE VERY MUCH WHILE WE WAIT FOR SOMEONE GOOD.
YES, YES, IT'S EXCELLENT!

I ALSO APPROVE, MISTY!

KEEP IN MIND THAT THE IMPORTANT THING IS TO PARTICIPATE. YOU JUST HAVE TO DARE TO DO IT. WHETHER IT'S TALKING OR SINGING IN ENGLISH, IT'S ONLY A MATTER OF TRYING, OF NOT BEING AFRAID OF LOOKING FOOLISH.

UNFORTUNATELY, ANTHONY AND I CAN'T BE THERE BECAUSE WE'RE WORKING, BUT OUR HEARTS WILL BE WITH YOU. IN ANY CASE, KATHLEEN, IT'S BEEN A REAL PLEASURE HAVING YOU WITH US IN OUR HOME.

AND HERE ARE SOME GOOD VIBRATIONS. I'VE BROUGHT YOU A LAST-MINUTE GUEST.
HELLO!

NOTHING BETTER THAN SOME ACCOMPANIMENT FOR SUCCESSFUL REHEARSALS! I'LL ALSO GIVE YOU SOME PRO TIPS, YOU'LL SEE.
THANKS, UNC!

WHOA!
WHOA!
WHOA!
YOU'RE IN TOP FORM.

CLIC

BRAVO, CHLOE! CONGRATU-LATIONS!

IT'S NOT NICE TO MAKE FUN OF ME, ETHAN! I'M JUST TRYING TO HELP YOU PRACTICE CORRECTLY.

I'M NOT MAKING FUN OF YOU. YOU REALLY HAVE A VERY PRETTY VOICE!

HE'S RIGHT! AND YOU TO KNOW THE WORDS WELL.
ANITHA'S NOT GOING TO BE HAPPY WHEN THE FINDTH OUT THAT THE NO LONGER HATH THE RIGHT THONG. HA, HA, HA!

WH--

OOPTH!

SLAM

NOW EVERYTHING'S RUINED!
MAYBE WE CAN CONVINCE LESLIE NOT TO SAY ANYTHING...
AGREEING WITH FATOUMATA! I'M GOING TO TALK TO HER!
PFFF!
YOU'LL TALK! SHE'LL NEVER LISTEN TO US. SHE'S LIKE A SHEEP FOLLOWING ANISSA. SHE TOOK THE NEW LYRICS. OF COURSE, SHE'LL TELL ANISSA EVERYTHING!
LESLIE, WAIT!
I KNOW YOU HEARD EVERYTHING. BUT DO YOU REALLY WANT TO FOLLOW YOUR FRIEND?
YOU AGREE WITH HOW SHE TREATS YOU?!
ASK YOURSELF.

The day of the show finally arrives...

OO! OO! WHERE'S THAT HANDSOME ENGLISH GUY HIDING?

I'VE LEARNED MY LYRICS COMPLETELY... I EVEN THOUGHT UP SOME SPECIAL CHOREOGRAPHY!
AH, NO, SORRY. ANOTHER SINGER'S GOING TO JOIN ME!

WHAT'S THIS GIBBERISH AGAIN... DO YOU UNDERSTAND ANYTHING?
...
WELL, NO...

LISTEN, STOP BEING A WIMP! YOU'RE GOING ONSTAGE WITH ME, PERIOD. THE TEACHERS DECIDED. ANYWAY, YOU'RE NOT GOING TO DISOBEY THEM?!
UP TO YOU!

HERE ARE THE STATEMENTS FROM THE STUDENTS YOU THREATENED AT THE AUDITION. IF MRS. PANIGOT AND MRS. ROBINSON SEE THIS LIST, YOU'LL BE KICKED OUT OF THE SHOW. MAYBE YOU'D RATHER GIVE UP, INSTEAD?

GRRRR... ANYWAY, I'M THE ONLY ONE WHO CAN PERFORM THAT SONG!

THAT SONG, YES! BUT WE CHOSE NEW LYRICS WITH A NEW PARTNER!

YOUR PITIFUL SHOW'S GOING TO BE A FLOP!
COME ON, GIRLS. LET'S LET THEM MAKE FOOLS OF THEM-SELVES!

GREAT BLUFFING, ETHAN! SO WHO ARE YOU GOING TO SING WITH IN THE END?
IT'S THE TRUTH. I'M GOING TO SING WITH YOU, CHLOE!

HUH?!

YOU KNOW THE WORDS, HAVE A PRETTY VOICE, AND WE'RE BOTH FRIENDS... YOU'RE PERFECT PERSON: YOU ALWAYS HAVE BEEN!

FRANKLY, I DON'T THINK I CAN DO IT! PLUS, IT'S IN FRONT OF LOTS OF PEOPLE...

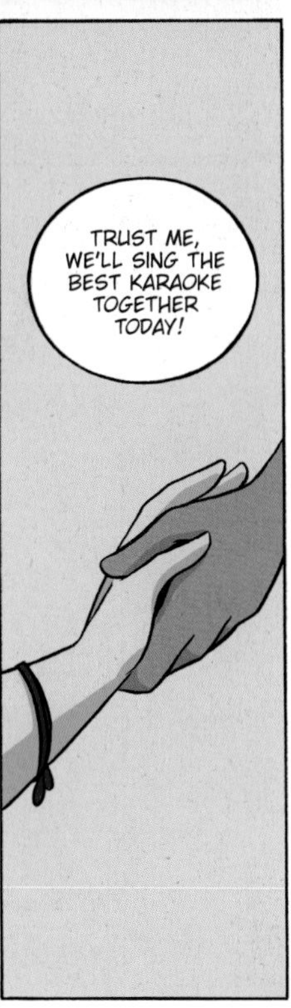
TRUST ME, WE'LL SING THE BEST KARAOKE TOGETHER TODAY!

THE ROOM'S ALREADY FULL...
EVERYTHING'S GOING TO GO WELL, SWEET CHLOE!
GOOD LUCK, MY FRIEND!
THREE
TWO
ONE...
GO!
IMAGINE THERE'S NO HEAVEN. IT'S EASY IF YOU TRY. NO HELL BELOW US. ABOVE US ONLY SKY...
IMAGINE ALL THE PEOPLE LIVING FOR TODAY...
I NEVER WOULD HAVE GUESSED SHE COULD SING SO WELL...

PROCHAINE CHANSON, NEXT SONG... POUR... FOR
OUR TEACHER, MRS. ROBINSON!
Wow, wow, wow
God bless you please, Mrs Robinson,
Heaven holds a place for those who pray,
Hey, hey, hey
Hey, hey, hey

Last name: Blin-Wood

First name: Chloe-Kathleen

Class: franco-anglais

Fact sheet England

n°3

Royauté

British monarchy

The system of government in the United Kingdom is still a hereditary monarchy, that is, there's a king who passes his title to his heirs, from generation to generation.
Very often, there are queens here, too, some of whom are very well known: Victoria, Elizabeth I, and currently Elizabeth II.

She seems very commanding when you don't know her, but actually she's very REGAL!

Oh yeah!!!

Musique

MUSIC

British music is listened to a lot in foreign countries and has many different cultural influences. Pop and rock'n'roll are the best known styles, though. Millions of people have danced to songs by groups such as the Beatles, the Rolling Stones, Queen, and the Spice Girls.

Uncle Steve is the first to know!

In England, we also have beautiful musical comedies.

Humour

British humor, often called, "English humor," commonly refers to a sophisticated form of humor characterized by its use of the absurd and nonsense, and by exploiting eccentricity.

I know someone who could use a bit of humor right now...

Heure du thé

tea time

Even though the English drink it at different times of the day, tea in the middle of the afternoon, "five o'clock tea," is a veritable ritual in Great Britain.
The seventh duchess of Bedford in the 19th century gradually started to invite her friends to share it. She started a fashion that took off rapidly and was very successful!

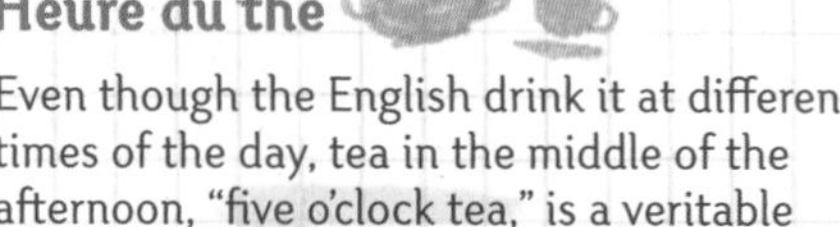

Being together with friends is heaven!
Good Vibration

Météo = Here, the weather's great!!!

weather

The myth of umbrellas has lasted for a long time in England!
Today, studies show, however, that it rains more in Paris, Rome, and Lisbon than in London. Except in June, July, and August, the amount of rain in the English capital is quite close to that in Madrid, the capital of Spain.

Best exchange students forever!

I REALLY DON'T WANT YOU TO GO...
I'M GOING TO MISS YOU A LOT, CHLOE!

OUR TIME TOGETHER WAS MAGIC! YOU'RE THE BEST EXCHANGE STUDENT IN THE WORLD!
YOU'RE THE BEST EXCHANGE STUDENT IN THE UNIVERSE!

IT'S HARD TO BELIEVE WE'VE ONLY KNOWN EACH OTHER FOR A WEEK... TO THINK THAT AT THE START WE COULDN'T TALK TO EACH OTHER.
I HOPE YOU TO COME TO ENGLAND SOON!

I'D REALLY LIKE--

GO ON! IT'S LOVE!

BYE, ETHAN...
YOU'RE EXTRAORDINARY, CHLOE! YOU'RE INTELLIGENT, CURIOUS... PRETTY... SO FRENCH!

BEEEEP
BEEEEEEEEP

I'LL NEVER FORGET THE TIME SPENT WITH YOU.

I'LL NEVER FORGET YOUR STAY WITH US EITHER...

OUR EXCHANGE STUDENTS WERE TOTALLY TERRIFIC!